AFTER

AN ANATOMY OF FRACTURE

BY DREW STARLING

PRAISE FOR
AFTER

Unsentimental speculative fiction that's wire-taut and emotionally rich. In Starling's post-apocalyptic novel with SF elements, a nameless messenger carries communications between survivor settlements in a dangerous American West.... Along the way, the author gets across a sense of fear of what lies around every corner and reveals the visible and invisible scars of the traumatized.
— KIRKUS REVIEWS

Drew Starling has created a delightful nightmare of imagery, prose, and characters to root for... Or against. Don't be afraid to slip into this post-apocalyptic tale of excellence.
— CINDY O'QUINN, BRAM STOKER AWARD®-WINNING AUTHOR

A bleak and brutal tale of one woman's fight for survival in a post-apocalyptic nightmare. With unforgettable imagery, Drew Starling delivers a tale of grief, courage, dread, and the best and the worst of human nature, combining Mad Max: Fury Road and War of the Worlds into one heart-pounding story.
— BEVERLEY LEE, AUTHOR *THE SUM OF YOUR FLESH*, AND *THE HOUSE OF LITTLE BONES*

With beautifully elegant prose, masterful world building and an unflinching and uncompromised vision, Drew Starling successfully whips this grief laden story into a frenzy of unbridled, visionary brilliance, where all its elements coalesce to make 'After' an exceptional piece of human centred, grief-riddled, dystopian brilliance.
— ROSS JEFFERY, BRAM STOKER AWARD-NOMINATED AUTHOR OF *I DIED TOO, BUT THEY HAVEN'T BURIED ME YET* AND *THE DEVIL'S POCKETBOOK*

A prose master truly in his element, Starling paints a harsh canvas equal parts beautiful and brutal. This post-apocalyptic tale of survival and acceptance deserves to be sipped and savored like a twelve-year bourbon.
— L.P. HERNANDEZ, AUTHOR OF *NO GODS, ONLY CHAOS*

With juicy prose, stunning imagery, and an imagined world that feels all too real, Starling's After is a bleak but beautiful slice of post-apocalyptic pie you'll want a second helping of.
— TIM MEYER, AUTHOR OF *MALIGNANT SUMMER* AND *LACUNA'S POINT*

Unequivocally haunting. Starling mixes McCarthy's '*The Road*' and Villeneuve's '*Arrival*' to deliver a PTSD-infused road trip where nothing good ever happens but hope is still chased. This book hurts to read, but must be read.
— STEVE STRED, *MULTIPLE AWARD NOMINATED AUTHOR OF MASTODON AND CHURN THE SOIL*

Starling paints a vivid portrait in cool grays and crimson reds; a stark contrast of bleakness and hope that presents a world that drains the will to live, then shows why we go on anyway. Terrifying, turbulent, and written with painstaking beauty, AFTER will break your heart and light a fire in the rubble.
— BRENNAN LAFARO, AUTHOR OF *I WILL ALWAYS FIND YOU*

After delivers a nasty combination of grief, terrifying aliens, the worst of human nature, and a brutal environment. However, despite the overwhelming horror, Drew Starling manages to inject small glimmers of hopefulness throughout the story. Fleeting bits of light in a world gone dark.
— C.M. FOREST, AWARD WINNING AUTHOR OF INFESTED

EERIE RIVER PUBLISHING
www. EerieRiverPublishing.com

Eerie River Publishing
www.EerieRiverPublishing.com
Kitchener, Ontario Canada

Subdivision of Eerie Ventures Ltd.

Paperback ISBN: 978-1-998112-40-1
Digital ISBN: 978-1-998112-39-5
Editor: Candace Nola and Austrian Spencer
Artwork Interior and Cover: Nathan Logan

Book Formatting by Michelle River of Eerie River Publishing

ALSO BY
DREW STARLING

THE BENSALEM FILES

SENTINEL: Book One (2021)
NOTHUS: Book Two (2022)

CONTENT WARNING

This book contains material that may be unsatisfying for some readers. For a full list of content warnings, visit the back of the book.

'I have spoken of the rich years when the rainfall was plentiful. But there were dry years too, and they put a terror on the valley.'

— JOHN STEINBECK

'You know, Burke, I don't know which species is worse.'

— ELAINE RIPLEY

FOR

CHAD M. GILLENWATER JR.

PART 1

AFTER

The woman lowered her binoculars and regarded the land through her own eyes. The road ahead graded slightly uphill, and it was flanked on both sides by desert, a pewter pigskin of earth and rock, barren save for the occasional shrub or patch of twisted grass. Over the foggy brim of the horizon, the road disappeared into a suffocating mountain mist that masked the red lands of the west.

After riding downhill for the better part of the morning, the change in depth marked her halfway point through the basin. A million years ago, surging torrents of water washed over the rubble upon which she stood. That ancient era and the one she now found herself in, here at the bottom of a dead river, wading not through water but the muck of her reality, shared little beyond their mutual emptiness of sentient life.

She put the binoculars into one of her two chrome saddlebags, mounted the bike, and twisted the ignition key. Before easing the clutch into first and hitting the throttle, she loosened the CO_2 converter strapped over her mouth so that it hung below her jaw like the abdomen of some mechanical tarantula.

It was a broken road, cracked and fissured from a decade of

neglect. Not the benign neglect that befalls so many things when their keepers lack the will or resources to maintain them, but a state of absolute despair, an erasure from the consciousness of all things living. She trundled forward, weaving the bike around shallow craters and gashes in the asphalt, and she rode slowly to minimize the risk of blowing a tire, bending a rim, or jolting the front suspension. Green signs with white print naming distances between cities from the old world whisked by her as she rode. She didn't look at them because they held no meaning anymore.

Riding out of the basin saw her onto a broad plateau coated with western wheatgrass. Soft winds tossed and rippled the reeds, effortlessly conducting their billions of independent bodies to move as one. At times, it seemed they bent away as her bike chewed up the arrow-straight road, cowering in her presence and united in their conspiracy.

Sunbeams fell upon the plain in the early afternoon, and as the clouds broke and the sun appeared, so too did myriad black floating disks of great diameter. The vessels of the invaders, made of materials unknown and arriving from some godless origin, bastardized the sky into a hysterical, polka-dot mosaic of black on azure blue that stretched on for eternity. They hung like obsidian cosmic chandeliers, some of them as large as cities, over every section of the globe, serving as an ever-present reminder of humanity's functional extinction. There was no place on the planet from which at least one of them could not be seen.

The woman rode on as the color of the asphalt abruptly shifted from an innocent gray to icy black, and though there was no change in atmosphere upon crossing into the disk's shadow, its sheer specter coated the land beneath it in a veil of oppression and despair. She dared not look up, only down, constantly analyzing the nuances of the road for any fault that might wreck the bike and strand her.

She rode through the shadow for miles, and only when a message board lodged between two copper-colored boulders appeared on the side of the road ahead did she downshift and roll to a stop. A perpendicular dirt road bisected the asphalt just behind it.

Before dismounting in a place where her breath would linger, she strapped the CO_2 converter tightly back over her nose and mouth and checked its mechanical bearing attached to her hip. Three green bars on the display told her the air she exhaled was being altered thoroughly enough to mask her presence. If those bars were red, or if she had no such device, they would smell her and they would find her and they would kill her.

The message board was a shiny piece of scrap metal, a jagged remnant of a lost civilization, chained to a pair of poles between the boulders. On it, six pieces of weather-beaten cloth had been lashed grid-wise with whatever string or tie wire the poster had available.

She read all the messages but untied only the two destined for Comm 971.

```
Lonnie Markum (comm 971)

Mother has fallen ill again and we done all we
can for her. Bad. Doc sayz three months max.
In much pain. Find next caravan to 445 if you
would like to see her. She would like to see
you.

Your sister, Michaela (445)

PS. How are things? You don't have to reply.
I know it's expecnsiv.

Purse: 1 lb jerked meat or 1 dzn potatoes.
Messenger's choice.
```

And:

```
To: Janis Witherspoon, Comm 971
```

From: Michelle Johnson, Comm 392

Dear J, I cannot tell you what a delight it was to receive your message. Yes, you are most welcome to stay with us. I'm sorry to hear things in 971 have taken a turn. I fear the same may happen any day here, but it has not happened yet. Our perimeter is well guarded and the sun still shines through the disks on bright days. So I am holding out hope and I am holding thoughts in my heart of seeing you again soon. Whether or not you get this message. Or whether or not you make it out here. Know you are so loved. You have been a treasure in my life, and when I want to go back in my mind, I remember the joy we shared before the war. I remember our late nights in college, our weddings, the births of our children. You have always been there for me and if I can be there for you, even if only for a little while, it would be my honor. Get here soon.

I had a best friend but she has come to pass

One I wish I could see now

You always remind me that memories will last

These arms reach out…

Yours,

M

Purse: Choice of materials from scrapyard OR 10-gal fuel OR nonperishables (negotiable)

After folding both messages and locking them in her saddlebag, she relieved herself behind the board and scanned the horizon. It was dead quiet out there on the plains, and all that moved in the sky was the speck of a lone bird drifting through the blue-gray distance.

She inched her converter down and munched on handfuls of a seed mix she kept in a worn plastic bag, holding her breath while she chewed and sliding the converter back over her nose and mouth to exhale. Two and a half of the four water bottles strapped to the saddlebags were full. She yanked the half-full bottle from its holster and gulped its contents before remounting the bike.

The road smoothed out over a wooded stretch made darker by the lengthening day and the dropping temperature. Untamed boughs of pine festooned over the asphalt, shepherding her into the chapel of their protection, some of them so low their needles, green and rich and strong, grazed her as she climbed from second to third gear. She rode on as the trees parted and the sun fell unceremoniously behind a wall of mountain fog, and the holes of sky not already black darkened to match the color of the disks. If she had looked up, she would not have seen a single star.

A flat and lush plot set within a community of aspens compelled her to stop. She heaved the bike off the road through a phalanx of ivory trunks, unfurled a large satchel tied to the back seat, and began to construct her fold-up tent.

One by one, she peeled off her articles of clothing, all of them plated in leather, keeping on only her undergarments and the military tags hanging from her neck. Inside the tent, she sat with her elbows on her knees and her palms gripping her shaved head. It was the woman's desire to fashion herself in a manner she deemed wholly unattractive, as the men in this world had great desire for any living woman, especially one without company. She pulled and massaged the skin covering her scalp, and she rubbed the pads of her fingers through the three-day-old stubble covering it. Outside, the aspen boughs billowed in the evening wind, their emerald leaves shimmering like thousands of little mirrors, while the faint coronas of fireflies pulsed through the tent's canvas and asked questions of the lengthening shadow.

A purple cloth pouch that she had brought in from her saddlebags lay in the corner of the tent. She didn't touch it and she didn't look at it, but that pouch emitted a white-hot pulse that pinged the fibers of her soul as she fell asleep.

Every so often, and especially at night, the disks would howl at each other like celestial coyotes in terrible conversation. They did so this night, and the woman rolled on her side and covered her exposed ear with her palm. Somewhere in those black and soulless saucers governing the sky existed intelligent beings communicating messages no earthling could fathom or interpret.

When their howling stopped, the woman rolled onto her back and closed her eyes. That night, as most, was a tightrope walk between sleep and waking, her lids rolling closed only for the howls of the disks to jerk them open again.

Just before dawn, she put her clothes back on and cleaned out her converter with a mouthful of recycled water. A dewy spring mist blurred the negative spaces behind the aspens into an aquamarine canvas. Birds and frogs and insects, all too small or flighty for the invaders to mind, sang as one in praise of a day that would be greener than the next. She saw no deer, no moose, no wolf, no bear. They were all gone. It had been at least five years since she'd last seen a fox.

The road was still damp from the mountain dawn. She took it slow, and as the sun began to bleed through a quilted sky, she swung the bike onto a thick vein of hard, yellow dirt slicing north. The trees fanned out, and the landscape morphed into a teal meadow brilliant and bright with dew enough to radiate under still overcast skies.

But the clouds retreated by mid-morning, and when those heinous disks appeared in the blue void above, out with them came a spectral moon that leered at her like the cotton eye of a blind man. She rode on as the meadow shriveled into a tableau of sagebrush and bunchgrass.

Beige and yellow hills formed around her, and as the day grew long, so too did their shadows, creeping around her like old ghosts, spilling into the silhouettes of the disks and blanketing the plain in a black cowl that belied the afternoon's early hour.

She rode on as dusk vanquished the daylight, and as the sun set to her left and the moon returned to her right, they seemed to briefly hang in unison, acknowledging each other above the disks before parting. By the time she flicked on the bike's headlight, the plain had become a barren and rocky basin of immeasurable expanse, littered only with errant boulders and flares of misfit weeds. The woman was microscopic in the twilight, a speck of stardust floating over a lunar crater. She laid a gloved hand over the dome gas tank cover between her legs, nearly caressing it, and whispered, "Almost." The yellow-white halogen on the front frame of the bike was the only light in the entire world.

She camped off-road under the vertical guard of a mesa's slope, and with only moonlight to aid her, cut down several knotted barbs of creosote bush and cast them over the tent and the bike to hide from aliens that would slice her open in sleep or humans that would do worse in waking.

Out here, there was no sound, not even the disks, save for a single dull groan of falling rock that belched forth from somewhere out of the dead throat of the mountains. It was cold, and her teeth chattered as she choked down sticks of jerky and meager gulps of water. The sight of scant, far-flung lights through her binoculars, the lights of Comm 971, did not warm her.

Sleep found the woman, and she woke stiff but rested to raindrops tap dancing on the tent. She laid there for a while before rinsing her converter with the remainder of her water and setting all four open bottles just outside the vestibule. With a ragged towel and the leather strap of the binoculars draped over her neck, she scampered in her undergarments and her converter up the wide slope of the mesa and bouldered on all fours to the peak. She sat down cross-legged, closed her eyes with a soft sigh, and wrenched her neck down to one shoulder, releasing cracks from the depths of her spine.

Yesterday's ride had caked her in yellow desert dust, and the exhausted flaps and pats she inflicted upon her clothing before bedding down did little to dislodge it. The rain washed over her. It cleansed her. Beads of clay colored water swam over her stubbly scalp. Once the towel was soaked through, she used it to wipe down her head, her neck, her arms, and her feet.

A magpie coasted over her shoulder and landed on the crown of a cactus, where it dug its beak furiously into its chest and shook off the rain before moving on. The woman raised the binoculars and watched the bird skirt south towards the wetlands, and not lowering them, spun to gaze again upon Comm 971. It had been cobbled out of scrap metal and rock under a highway overpass, a dark and dilapidated wart jutting into a marbled gray sky.

She climbed down the mesa, dressed, packed up, and swam her arms through a thick, military-issue poncho stuffed in the bottom of the saddlebag. It, like the rain, poured off her, the sleeves spilling well past her hands. Her converter-clad head was miniscule in the cavern of its hood, and she lashed it around her forehead with twine to keep it from her face.

The rain grew heavier. By the time Comm 971 had drawn within naked sight, any part of her not covered by the poncho was soaked, and as she trundled cautiously ahead in first gear, a torrent of yellow mud spewed from the back tire like projectile vomit.

All the old roads leading to the comm had been sabotaged by bandits: people who preyed on the weak and gentle-hearted for food, supplies, and other things that satiated the urges of men. Its vicinity looked like the aftermath of an explosion, with hunks of old metal, wood, barbed wire, and pulverized vehicles scattered about. Several empty tents stood pitched nearer to the entrance, and several more lay ripped and ruined on the ground.

The walls of the place were mountains of chum from the old world — steel and concrete sandwiched in with whatever else they could find — all of it smashed together and packed tight with mud. Mud, that in the rain made Comm 971 appear to be crying, brown streaks of sadness running down its face.

It had one door: a towering slice of old plane fuselage, now rusted out and branded a thousand times over with epitaphs in graffiti. Dominating this canvas of last words, a crimson-colored plea screamed its stark warning—NO FOOD NOTHING TO ROB—drowning out all other voices etched upon the metal. If one could peel back those words and uncover the underlying layers, the glyphs and cries narrating Comm 971's decline would be revealed. Messages of white defeat, yellow despair and grief, black anger, and, at the very bottom of it all, blood-red fear.

With the back of a gloved fist, she rapped on the aluminum monolith. A small sliding window about head height had been carved right out of it, and she peered through for a moment before pounding on the door again.

"Hello?"

No answer. Nothing in the window.

She untied the twine around her head and pulled her hood over her eyes as the rain continued to batter her and her bike. Out to the east, a reluctant white stain of sunlight suffused the hills, and to the west, the most severe grouping of rain clouds now strangled the snowy tips of the mountains. Thousands of raindrops pinging the door muffled another knock, and a frustrated kick.

She retrieved a cement-crusted wand of rebar and smacked it repeatedly against the door. The echo of her provocations rang up the length of the walls and fell back down.

Suddenly, the sliding window jerked open, and a voice called back to her. "Who are you?"

The woman tossed the rebar aside. "I'm a messenger. Do you still have a desk here?"

The phantom voice behind the window was old and thin, the gender of its bearer indeterminate. Only the lower half of their face was visible, and most of it was obscured by a low-tech converter held on by string. "We ain't got no desk anymore."

"Of course not. Can you at least let me in? I have messages for two of your people."

The little window crashed shut, and as if compelled by magic, one edge of the fuselage crept slowly back, chains behind it rattling.

What opened before her was summarily a single chamber, a murky gray cave lit by oil lamps and candles hanging from hooks bolted to the bottom of the old overpass. Pouches of rain fell in through gaps in the roof. Shacks sharing no visual commonality besides their ugliness lined the interior perimeter, most of them built out of tin and anonymous rubble. There was no firepit or organized center, just more piles of dirty and broken things, time capsules shattered and spilled into a world that no longer had use for their contents. The air stank of wet metal.

At least two dozen residents had come out to see her, and the silent repose in which they stood, rag clad and eyes blazoned, could have been confused for a beautiful calmness. They were a people arraigned, a clan discarded by all powers of the natural world, both human and alien alike. Some of them held hands.

The woman removed her hood and stepped among them, poncho shimmering with rain and dragging behind her like the cape of some comic evildoer. With one hand, she corralled the poncho's apron and reached into her pocket.

"I'm a messenger," she said, holding the messages aloft as if salvation should emanate from them. "Is there a Janis Witherspoon here?"

No one moved.

"Is there a Janis Witherspoon here?" she repeated. Her converter, like all converters, warped her voice through a sort of muffled filter, edging away hard consonants and softening vowels.

The little old doorkeeper materialized under her raised elbow. "She left with the last caravan north."

"212," someone else said.

The woman nodded.

A young girl emerged from the crowd, cheeks sunken and eyes bearing the vacantness of starvation under a rat's nest of dreadlocked hair. She wore a single shroud of cloth and no shoes, and she approached the woman slowly as if an arbiter of pure despair, the legatee of some cursed generational contract.

"Did you bring food?" said the girl. The converter she wore was sized for a head much larger.

The woman looked down at the girl but spoke loud enough for all to hear her. "Was hoping you might have some for me."

Someone towards the back of the crowd coughed. Everyone stared. Their hollow eyes were like vectors to mankind's most terroristic histories, memories of hells once locked in the bowels of a collective unconscious, now regurgitated upon her. They stared at her from a state of humanity reduced, minds erased, and hearts pulverized. A single, sentient mass contemplating its annihilation.

"Okay," the woman said to the crowd. "How about a Lonnie? Brother of Michaela?"

A rail thin man with spindly white beard hairs pouring out of his converter gestured to a shack built out of the eastward wall.

"He's over there?" the woman asked.

When the man didn't reply, she looked down at the doorkeeper, still by her side. They were admiring the bike.

"Hey," the woman said, snapping their dark little eyes, beady like pebbles, back on her. "Is Lonnie back there?"

"Yeah."

She wheeled the bike over to the shack, and the crowd, seemingly compelled by some heliotropic instinct, craned their necks in observation of even her most insignificant movements.

A dirty curtain, maybe an old bed sheet, hung from a rod straddling two walls of rusted out corrugated tin. When she pulled the curtain back, a rank and rotting stench wafted over her.

"Oh," she said. "Oh, Jesus."

The inside of the shack was the very picture of squalor. Not an inch of natural floor was visible, only a sea of garbage. Nor was there any light or furniture, save a cot shrouded in darkness. An off-colored liquid dripped from the ceiling. The smell was so bad she had to clamp a ponchoed elbow over her converter.

An obese man sat with his hands on his knees on the floor in the corner. Sweat poured off him, matting his stringy hair to his forehead and fogging his glasses such that his eyes were completely invisible. His breathing was loud and labored, and the sheer grip of the converter straps across his bloated face erased any distinction between chin and neck. He was Caucasian but the skin on his hands and forearms was brown, from sun or dirt or both, and his calves and ankles were cherry-colored balloons swollen with hypertension and disease. All twenty of his nails were crusted black with dirt. He was looking at the cot.

"Lonnie?" she said.

He nodded.

With an elbow still over her converter, she tiptoed through the filth and offered him the message. His arm shook, weak under fat and atrophied muscle, and when he took the message, it swung back down like a pendulum. He read while the woman looked at the cot.

A sliver of light from outside lit a diagonal streak of the cot's occupant, a man positioned just so that the bloody bandages of one amputated arm and one amputated leg were exposed. He was old. Naked and frail, gray and crusty, dying if not already dead. Eyes closed. Crumbling converter strapped over his nose and mouth. Two cockroaches positioned outward like maniacal eyebrows gnawed on the arm wound.

"What's wrong with this man? Don't tell me you—"

"I want to see her." Lonnie's voice was high and thin, almost feminine, a wraith in the darkness and the stink.

"What?"

"I'll never see her again."

She pointed to the message. "Do you know how the signature field works there? You sign that so I can get my purse from the sender. You have anything to write with?"

"Can you take me?"

"What?"

"Can you take me to see her?"

She scoffed. "That's not how this works."

He let his knees collapse, spilling his mostly exposed great and hairy gut over his lap. "How will I get there?"

"I have no idea. That's not my area."

"How did you get here?"

"Do you have anything to write with or not?"

He shook his head.

"Jesus Christ," she said, retreating, but stopped with the curtain pulled back. "You'd be a lot better off just killing that man. It's evil what you're doing to him."

"He told us we could."

She scoffed and threw the curtain shut behind her.

Orange afternoon light knifed through the gaps in Comm 971's roof, reddening for a brief time before fading with the onset of evening.

The woman removed her poncho and walked between the shacks and bartered away half of her food to the emaciated man for three gallons of fuel. While inside his shack, she tried not to gawk at the twisted child strapped to a wheeled board behind him. Compulsively, the boy pushed himself back and forth across the dirt with a dangling hand, and while his head was pointed in her direction, his eyes, hollow and horrible, clung to the caving ceiling above them.

She then took up behind Lonnie's and laid down with her head against the bike's front tire. She didn't bother with the tent, opting to directly intercept the stares of the oft curious residents with gazes of her own.

The comm was still when night came. Muffled cries, soft like a little girl's, bled out from Lonnie's shack before quieting, while a cacophony of groans and hacking coughs came from the others. The woman fell asleep to the rhythm of drops pinging an empty pipe somewhere, the purple pouch on her stomach under interlocked fingers.

She dreamed of a young boy. He had her eyes and his father's nose and lips. Back and forth, the boy clicked an umbrella open and shut. The sun was shining. Her husband came in from the other room and left. There were other people in the house. They were nervous. The boy said something but she couldn't make it out. It wasn't raining yet.

When the day's first light seeped in, she rose and walked the bike in covert solitude to the fuselage door. The doorkeeper sat on a metal box under the wall, a sort of gutter-bound concierge. They called out to the woman. "We have somethin' for you."

Two small men, frowning and ragged, approached the woman from behind while the doorkeeper looked on. One of the men was in shorts and a tee shirt, the other wore a heavy parka. The woman slid her hand over the saddlebag latch, crept two fingers in, and curled the gun closer.

"Is there any way for you to take Lonnie to 445?" said the one in the parka.

She sighed and let go of the gun. "Sorry. This bike's barely big enough for me."

"What if you walked?"

She studied them both for a moment. "No way."

The one in the tee shirt stepped forward and revealed a shining motorcycle helmet. "Would you do it for this?"

She studied the helmet, ran a finger along its edges, tested its give. Then she gave it back to him. "I'm gonna need more than that."

His voice was softer now. "We really don't have a lot here. We—"

"We thought you might like it," said the doorkeeper.

"I'm sorry. He's too big to fit on the bike and it's too dangerous to walk. The helmet's nice, but I'm not risking my life for it." She mounted the bike. "Or for him."

The man in the parka cleared his throat. "Lonnie doesn't have a lot of time left."

She squinted at him.

"He was too embarrassed to tell you because he thought you were mad at him. It would be a one-way trip."

The doorkeeper shrugged. "There hasn't been a sighting out east in weeks."

"What about the Crone?" said the woman.

"There's nothing left for her here."

The woman turned to the doorkeeper. "Sounds like you don't know the Crone."

"I've known every hell you can imagine."

Beyond the group at the door, a middle-aged woman huddled over a pile of what appeared to be thin strips of dried meat. She doled them out to several children crouched patiently around her, and she whispered as she did so. Some of the children, starving as they were, seemed reluctant to partake. One of them began to cry. The woman watched them.

"All right. Fine. Go get him."

It took three and a half days to reach Comm 445.

Relentless rain on the first day forced them eastward on foot. Save for Lonnie's calls for breaks, of which there were many, they said little to each other over the rain. The woman huffed and scoffed that evening as she organized her mud-soaked belongings, and it took her twice as long as it usually did to set up the tent. Lonnie brought little in the way of luggage, all his possessions fitting into a backpack that he kept strapped to his great bulk until they camped. He didn't ask to share the tent and she didn't offer. The black disks of the invaders were quiet again. Some believed they howled less in the rain, but no one was sure.

On the second day, the rain eased to a drizzle, and ragged clouds followed them through a mountain pass scalded deep into the earth. The two of them were like insects as they inched through the massive valley. Looming above, blood-orange layers of cut rock rose like cosmic stairs, pathways that might lead to a more placid timeline where nothing like this ever happened. Yet here, on an empty and decaying highway, the pass served only as a reminder of man's dominance for a brief time.

When the road dried, the woman managed to mount the bike by letting Lonnie fill the entire seat while she stood on the foot pegs and drove at a snail's pace in first gear. He asked about her that night — her family, her past — but she ignored him and covered her ears as the disks howled. They were loud, their moans cold and piercing. There was an undeniable language in those cries, and although earthly attempts at translation were purely speculative, the jarring patterns of their range and nuance seemed to convey feelings incompatible with human understanding.

The third day, clear and bright, brought them through an arcadia of wooded hills. They rode through pines, through aspens, through oaks and birches, and when they camped in the shadows of the wood, they saw lamps from Comm 445 far off in the green glow of the night.

Lonnie asked if they could build a fire.

"No," said the woman. "If we get seen, there's no way you'll be able to escape them, and I'm not going to protect you. I'm sorry to put it that way."

"I'm so cold," he said, teeth chattering. He hadn't changed clothes since they left the comm. "I just want to see her."

"You take the tent tonight. I don't want either of us doing anything stupid when we're this close." She rose, standing over him. "Deal?"

He nodded and crept inside.

The forest teemed with microscopic symphonies as the darkness washed over the land. When sunlight eked through the boughs above them, Lonnie was snoring and sighing through his converter while a charismatic group of white-throated sparrows chirped and flitted through the shrubs, jumping more than flying. A woodpecker tapped away in the nameless distance.

The woman laid in a bed of tall grass by the tent and held the purple pouch in silence, rubbing a thumb over its contours. Her eyes were open but distant and unmoving, almost lost, and she was very still.

In recent times, the comms that prospered were the ones cradled in natural rock or fortified on flatlands by concentric sets of man-made walls. Comm 445 touted the latter, and it doubly benefited from its position among a fortress of barrel-trunked evergreens. Well outside its outermost wall, lookout stations — lightweight wooden stands high in the trees — were connected by zip lines that allowed sentries to alert troops stationed within the garrison.

The woman waved to one as she and Lonnie passed, twisting her neck to the sky and flicking a wrist at a camouflaged figure peering back at her through binoculars. Not an inch of the sentry's skin was visible, their body wrapped in form-fitting brown and dark green clothes. Even their converter had been painted to match the wilderness.

"Let me do the talking," she said as slivers of the outermost wall materialized between the trees.

It was built from the same thick timbers standing proud around it, dozens of them stacked horizontally, bound with chains and wrapped in miles of angry-looking barbed wire. Three machine-gun clad guards, all in the same camo as the sentry, milled around a narrow gap in the wall. None of them raised their guns, but Lonnie still put his hands in the air. The woman guided them back down while handing the guards a leather billfold. The guard examined it.

"And who is that?" said the guard, nodding Lonnie's way.

She reached into her pocket and gave the guard the message. "His name's Lonnie. He's here to see his dying mother. His sister's name is written there."

The guard took it and read it. "He's the recipient, not the bounty."

"I know. I know this is against protocol."

"Does he have papers?"

Two more guards snuck out of the gap in the wall and joined the three already there. One of them looked up and whistled loudly to a sentry in the trees, and when the sentry turned around, the guard on the ground rattled off a series of vigorous hand signs.

"No, no," said the woman. "We're alone."

"If he doesn't have papers, we can't let him in."

"I'll sponsor him until we get to the desk."

The guard gave Lonnie a long, hard look and then walked back to the woman. "Thought there was no one left at 971. How the hell did you get him here?"

"It wasn't easy," she said.

"Is my mother here?" Lonnie said. Unlike the woman and the guards, Lonnie was completely drenched in sweat. His intense stench — moldy, oniony — was palpable to the guards, such that one recoiled in disgust. Somehow, spending three days in the elements had turned his skin even paler, giving him a blue and sickly appearance.

The guard waved them on.

The second wall was just a few dozen feet away and ran parallel to the first. Bunkers were carved out of its side where guards stood and talked and waited to be called upon to fight. By design, the gap leading to the third wall was nearly a hundred yards away, forcing intruders — man or alien — down a curving corridor of ballistic torture, as evidenced by splintered gashes, flowering smoke stains, and patches of dried blood slathered across the timbers.

A pair of old Toyota sedans with their tops sliced off passed on the left, each carrying a mix of guards and civilians armed with all manner of guns, one with a hand draped over a thick-barreled anti-tank missile launcher set on his shoulder. Other people passed on foot and gazed at them, chattering and shuffling over the packed dirt floor.

"Will you be able to find your family on your own?" the woman said as the gap in the second wall came into view up ahead.

"Where do I go?"

She pointed behind him. "Go down that side and turn right when you see the next gap. There should be a civilian checkpoint right inside and you should ask them where your family is."

"But the guard said I needed papers. What if—"

"You're good." She was already on her bike, revving the engine.

Lonnie looked up at a disk-filled sky. There was one right overhead, coating the comm in an odd noonday shadow. He shivered.

The woman rounded the bank of the innermost wall through a rookery of tents, shacks, barracks, and armories. A handful of teenagers were crouched low in the green maze of a vegetable garden, waddling like ducks as they nurtured their crops. She rode on as the clangs of a blacksmith cut through the buzz of her engine, and she did not return the idle glances of soldiers and civilians as she passed.

She parked beside a large wooden desk set under an awning strung up to an open shipping container. Something clamored inside the container and a voice called out.

"Just a minute."

The voice was a man's, the acoustics of the shipping container giving it artificial boldness and shape. The woman retrieved several messages from her saddlebags and piled them on the desk, then waited until the man emerged. He carried a box of tools in both arms, and he heaved it onto the desk with a metallic thud. He was a tall man, broad with drooping shoulders, and he wore an old pea coat and even older jeans.

She fanned out her stack of messages so that all were visible under her fingertips. "Hey, Regis. Redeeming these."

Regis chuckled and picked up the one closest to him. "Nice to see you, too. You've been busy."

"Better busy than dead."

He paused for a moment. "Not always so sure about that."

One by one he examined the messages, each time moving them to a box under the desk and then scribbling in a notebook.

"How long you here for?" he said, not looking up.

"Just the night."

He looked up at her and stopped writing. "Just the night?"

"There's a repair purse waiting for me at 880."

"You sure? That one ain't goin' anywhere."

"Yeah. I'm sure."

He shook his head. "There's been some trouble out that way. A lot of sightings. Why don't you stay a few days? Let it cool down. We can fix you up here."

The woman gazed into the shipping container, then back at the bustling street, then down at the desk. Anywhere but Regis' inquiring eyes.

"I can't fill this one," Regis said, pushing Lonnie's message back across the desk to her.

She scoffed. "I'm not getting nothing for that."

"There's no sig."

"I delivered his ass here."

He chuckled. "You did that out of the kindness of your still-beating heart. Cosmic brownie points."

"Why don't you help me out with the bike? I'm in desperate need of a new radiator. Starter, too. You've gotta have something I can look at."

"What about that repair purse you're all hot and bothered about?"

She finally looked at him. "Come on."

He sighed and squinted at the bike. "What is she again?"

"Suzuki GSXR 600. 2025."

"Poor old girl."

"She's not old and she's not poor."

He walked around to the bike and crouched beside it and peered into the engine. "You should get some fairing for this thing."

"You have some?"

"Oh, sure. I think there's some in there next to the beach chairs. Under the martini glasses." Laugh lines splintered across his converter-clad face.

"You don't even have a radiator, do you?"

He rose and looked at her, wiping his hands. "Give me a couple days and I will."

The chug of another motorcycle began to build behind them, a roaring rumble dripping with bass, unlike the high-octane buzz of the woman's.

"What about bitter grass?" she said. "I know you've got that."

Regis was already halfway back to the shipping container as she asked the question.

An old chopper-style Harley Davidson pulled up. The man who dismounted was small in stature, dressed in robes and riding leathers. He donned a head wrap instead of a helmet, and his eyes were dark and deep, like black stars. He took up a place several feet behind her and clasped his hands, robes billowing as his arms moved.

"Hello," he said to her, nodding reverently.

The woman didn't turn around. "Hey, Gaff."

"Long time no see," Gaff said, not moving. His voice was gruff and weathered, as if his throat had been run rough with sandpaper.

Regis returned with a fuel tank dangling from one hand and a small cardboard box propped on his other shoulder. He put the items on the desk. "Okay. Five gallons of fuel. Screwdriver set. Box of 9mm rounds. There's potatoes and apples together in this bag. You can probably trade those for seed mix or magpie jerky or whatever your twiggy ass subsists on at the bodega." He then tweezed an orange medicine bottle from the inside pocket of his pea coat. He held it aloft for a moment before offering it, drawing her eyes toward his. "And this is from me. On the house."

The woman released a heavy breath. "Damn, Regis. You're a lifesaver."

"But you take it easy on yourself now, okay? It won't fix anything. You'll wake up and you'll still be here." He pointed to the disk over them. "They'll still be here."

"I know. I know where I am. Thank you, Regis."

She took the bottle and stuffed it into her sleeve, and she didn't retrieve it until late that evening while sitting at a community plaza in the center of the comm.

The faces of those around the plaza's fire were bathed in orange firelight. Two men operated a small grill set atop the flames and pieced together kebabs with bits of squash, mushrooms, and various peppers. A young, dreadlocked woman sat on the hood of a car and strummed a guitar. A soldier shared a meal with his young family and bounced a toddler on his knee. Each time one of them took a bite, they peeled up their converters and slipped the food quickly into their mouths, chewing with their converters back on. The woman took out her binoculars to study an old man reading a book. He sat perfectly still, shadows from the fire dancing across his forehead.

A ragged man cautiously approached her. He wore an oversized pink sweater riddled with holes and smeared with dirt, and he rubbed his hands and blinked his dreary, red-rimmed eyes. "Excuse me?"

The woman regarded him with no great enthusiasm.

"I—I heard you at the desk earlier. I'm sorry for snooping. You're a messenger, right?"

"Yes, but I don't take personal requests. You'll have to post it to a public board or coordinate with the desk."

So filthy was the man's sweater that spills of dirt fluttered down with each soft step, each arm gesture. He stopped a fair distance away from her, almost cowering.

"I, uh, I don't need a message delivery. I was actually hoping you could help me find my son."

"Oh, no, I don't do that."

"Please. I have nothing. I have no family, no possessions. My little son was all I had and now he's gone. Taken from me."

She leaned back on her elbows and squinted at him.

"I'd just ask that you keep an eye out for him. I want him back so bad. I'd do anything to see him again."

"What's he look like?"

The man came to life. "Oh!" He held out a hand next to his hipline. "About this tall, I suppose. Sandy blond hair. One green eye and one blue. There's no other eyes like his, you see? They're the most special eyes."

"What's his name?"

"He answers to Mickey. His sister had this Mickey Mouse book. After she died, he became obsessed with it. He would look at the pictures and turn the pages until they were ragged. He loved it so much he wanted me to call him Mickey. So of course, I called him that."

"How'd you lose him then?"

"We were outside the walls gathering mushrooms in the early morning like we usually do. Just the two of us. Well, a few days ago, he drifted out of my sight and... and he was just gone. I heard something shuffle in the woods by the road. I told him not to go by the road."

"Did he run away?"

"No. No, ma'am. He's all I have and I'm all he has. He's my little partner, you see. We're partners in this together. He's just five years old. Follows me around everywhere. Oh God, I love him more than anything." Something inside the man appeared to collapse, his shoulders dropping and his voice sinking. Tears welled in his eyes. "His mother is gone, and we lost his sister just last year, you see? Despite it all, despite all this, he's such a happy and sweet kid."

"So, he just walked off?"

"No. He must have been taken."

"The guards would have seen someone, though."

"There's a lot they don't see up in the treetops." He leaned in close and grew quiet, afraid even the ground might hear him. "The Crone's people have been here. I think those Motherless snuck here and took him. Oh, I can't bear the thought! Mickey is the fourth child gone missing since winter."

The woman leaned forward and nodded slowly. "I don't fuck with the Crone."

His head sank. "Do you think... do you think you'll go look for him?"

"I'm not a P.I. I'm a messenger. But I'll keep an eye out. If I find him, I know where to take him, but I'm not going to go searching for him. You could commission a tracker or merc to do that."

"I don't have any money to pay for one. I don't have anything."

She opened the medicine bottle. "What's your name?"

"My name?"

"Yes."

"Jonah. My name's Jonah.

"Good luck, Jonah. For what it's worth, I know what this feels like."

They looked at each other for a long time until Jonah nodded and slunk back to the shadowy corridors between the shacks.

She tapped the side of the orange medicine bottle with her index finger. Several leafy bulbs fell out, and she packed three of them into a small pipe and smoked it in the same manner she ate — lifting her converter only to inhale. The guitar player stopped and looked up to the sky, gazing, wondering.

The woman stretched out her legs and fell asleep with the purple pouch in her hands.

And she was seated at a conference table that seemed to go on for miles in either direction. Everyone around it wore a navy-blue uniform and a grave expression.

"They are terminal," a commanding voice said. "They are lethal. They are total. There is no compromise, no communication. They are highly organized and there is no uncertainty in their actions. Carried out with zero hesitation."

One of the men at the table got up and began to cry. The woman followed him into another room, a room infinitely dark. His cries morphed into that of an infant's, wicked wails piercing the night, and the baby was lying naked on an operating table. She approached. Part of the baby's skull was broken, caved in as if someone had dug a fingernail in and begun to peel it open like an orange. The woman tried to repair the baby's skull, at one point accidentally breaking off a flake and setting it aside. The baby only cried harder. Someone entered the room and tried to take the baby away, but the woman wouldn't let them. The baby's cries flattened out into a single morbid and penetrating scream that woke her.

The raw glare of the comm's floodlights bathed the plaza in a cold, bluish light, a cryptic color both corporal and remote. From here, in the center of the comm, the shuffle of mobilizing soldiers on the perimeter was a soft, almost decorative sound, not unlike a crackling fire or the squawk of an errant crow.

But their voices grew, and their pace began to quicken. One of them shouted — and then fired.

She sat up just as the first wave of bullets rang out. Dozens of them, lightning fast, semi-automatic. A booming mortar blast followed by another. A guard yelled, a woman screamed, sentries zipped down their lines towards the point of the attack.

And a screech bellowed by a creature from hell itself split the night.

What came next wasn't an earthquake, but a calamitous crash into the outer wall that sent a shockwave through the comm. Interior guards poured into the plaza and urged calm to those sleeping and sitting. The people obeyed. They obeyed because they knew what to do. Anyone still living had gone through this before, some hundreds of times, and they knew there was nothing that could be done besides wait. If the walls were sturdy and the munitions were loaded and the soldiers were willing to lay down their lives, the sun would rise again for those trapped inside. But if any of these conditions were not met, the invaders would enter and—

You could see it written on the faces of every terrified man, woman, and child in the plaza. They didn't scurry in an attempt to grab a weapon or to hide. Instead, they huddled close to whoever or whatever they held most dear in their fractured world. Some of them — the families, especially — clung to each other. The children cried. Others simply closed their eyes, recalling a world more preferable to such an impossible present.

And then there were those who had nothing. Not a person, not a thing, not a memory in the world to hold on to. Their faces were abstract and vacant. They looked at nothing, thought about nothing, and they stared out into the void while decoupling themselves from their expression of life. They only wished that it would be over soon. Some even welcomed it.

When at last morning came, civilians gathered the dead soldiers and tended to the wounded. Commanders surveyed the damage while crews cleaned and repaired what they could. The young guitar player had to be restrained from diving into the pile of fresh dead. Fists balled, knees driving, heartbroken, she unleashed screams that scraped the heavens. At one point, the man carrying her lover's stretcher lost his grip, spilling the headless corpse into the street and laying the young woman's state to even greater ruin.

The woman did not look at her as she rode by, nor did she look at the bloodstained ground between the walls or the damaged timbers on either side of her. She didn't look at anything. She just rode.

She took the road south, riding back across the plain and the river basin, and by early afternoon, had reached the message board. After removing a message bound for Comm 332, she rehung the one for Janis Witherspoon after scratching out "971" and writing "212".

The basin was silent. If there was a single sound left in the world, no object of matter — living or inanimate — would have known it. She stood there and ate an apple and some jerky she had traded for the potatoes, and then she rode west, passing again through fields and sleepy pine stands.

When the road twisted around a blunted rock face that hid the terrain ahead, she slowed and glanced over the newly exposed plateau, and upon seeing the invaders, jerked the bike off the road so hard she nearly spilled it. She retrieved the binoculars from her saddlebags and crouched behind the bike.

From this distance, they were two shadowy, ambiguous blobs roughly a hundred yards away, but through the binoculars, they were those armor-plated, four-legged, blood-colored hellions. They fed on something red in the grass, clapping their clawed limbs against the ground, whipping their massive, flower-like mouths up and down, and emitting soft screeches to themselves, to each other, or to some wholly other diabolical thing.

She watched them, she waited, and she didn't move. Hours passed, but they did not, and neither did the stratus clouds ruffling high above the disks. She sat behind the bike, leaning against it and facing them, and she waited.

Then they moved, and they moved fast. Towards her. They bounded over the yellow plateau, each of their horrendous and double-jointed legs hitting the ground one at a time, giving them the appearance of headless raving mad horses.

She fumbled with the keys. When she turned the ignition, all the bike offered was a dull electrical hum.

"No. Fuck no."

They were closer now, bounding at a speed that peeled the four panels of their mouths back over their heads, revealing toothless, endlessly black, wet throats. A flock of birds perched on a bone-dry power line fled in all directions as they galloped under it.

She ripped open the seat cover with such strength and panic that the hinge broke and it flew clear across the road. The contents of her repair kit jangled as she fished for the screwdriver set. When she finally retrieved it, she engaged the clutch with her left hand, pinned a screwdriver's metal across both battery terminals with her knee, hit the starter button with her right hand, and the engine thrust on.

By now, the invaders had closed more than half the distance. They rampaged towards her over land they had long since conquered, crazed like members of a cavalry still blood lusting after the battle had been won. Their screeches were no longer soft, but maddening banshee cries, motivated by some twisted mixture of instinct, hunger, and incandescent rage. She didn't bother fixing the seat cover. She just sat on the open frame, throttled the gas, and flew back the way she came.

The invaders stampeded in pursuit. But just as the highway's bend erased nearly all sight of the road behind her, a smudge of purple grazed through the rear-view mirror. She whipped the bike one hundred and eighty degrees and accelerated towards them, towards the purple pouch in the middle of the road. The bike's gauge cluster flashed orange in mechanical alarm, but she did not heed its protest.

Collision imminent, all eight of the invaders' collective limbs leapt off the ground to pounce, but a split-second before they made contact, she jerked the bike off the road and into the dust, and then quickly back onto the road. She didn't stop. She didn't even slow down. She accelerated as she crossed her left hand to the right-side handlebar, leaned down to the ground, and swiped the pouch in her open right hand.

The bike choked and teetered as it blazed back through the foothills. The heat coming off the chassis was so great it began to burn her. She retraced her path through the plain and didn't look back until she reached the edge of the forest, and even then, still didn't slow down. She stood on the foot pegs to evade the scalding dome and the wrath of the broken shocks.

An early afternoon sun had crested through a disk in the southern sky by the time she finally dismounted at the message board. She climbed a boulder and scanned the horizon through her binoculars. The perpendicular dirt road behind the board led through miles of barren plain in both directions, but one end appeared to lead to a small and shapeless body of water. Tiny specs of sage shrubs and patchy green fields lined its perimeter. Without exhaling, she took off her converter and massaged the flesh around her jaw, and then put her converter back on. She looked at the bike, seatless and steaming.

As she rode slowly towards the water, her eyes did not waver from the shrub line until the bike's engine died about a half mile from her destination. She wheeled it several hundred yards off the road and left it on its side in the grass, and she took with her two water bottles and a small revolver from her saddlebag. The water was a man-made reservoir whose far bank funneled into a thin stream that ribboned through the prairie. One of its walls had collapsed, creating a murky shoreline where fresh grass crept up towards the plain.

Before she could bend her knees to crouch down to the water, a sharp glint of light flashed through her sight line. A man stood aiming a shotgun barrel straight at her.

"Hey now!" The woman stabbed her hands into the air. "I'm not an enemy. I need help."

"Who are you? What do you need?" said the man.

"My motorcycle's busted. It's back there. I just rode towards the water, hoping to find someone."

"Well, you found someone." He was dressed head-to-toe in an eclectic tunic stitched together from various leathers, cloths, and the furs of small rodents. A thick, red beard cupped an even redder face topped with scraggly hair down to his shoulders. Deep cracks ran lengthwise across his temples and parallel to his blue converter straps.

He nodded and lowered the gun. "I'm Elijah."

The woman nodded back. "You got any motor oil, Elijah?"

"Yeah. I do. What will you give me for it?"

"What do you want?"

With the shotgun's muzzle on the ground and both hands leaning down on its recoil pad, Elijah looked like some aboriginal cult leader contemplating judgment of a wayward disciple. "Did you see any?"

She nodded. "Two of them. Half a day's ride to the north."

"Where you comin' from?"

"Comm 445. I'm a messenger by trade."

He took a long look at her. "What're you working with? 'Bout a 600-cc engine?"

"Yeah. Yeah, actually. How did you know?"

"I could hear it."

"You know your bikes. So, I'm guessing you really do have that motor oil."

"Think I got some synthetic lyin' around."

"Close?"

He slung the rifle over his shoulder and pointed behind him. "Downstream. Come on, I'll take you to my place."

"Hey." She lowered her hands. "If you get squirrely with me, I'll kill you."

Elijah laughed and produced a framed photograph from inside his tunic and handed it to her. In it, he was twenty years younger, draped in a tropical setting with blazing white sand and thick palm trees, and he was kissing another man on the lips. Although time and light and sorrow had faded the picture's colors into a stale sienna, the fire in his young eyes had not dimmed.

Sans bike, she followed him downstream to a grove of white pines nestled under the ledge of a craggy rock face. A hut lay just beneath the slope and tucked behind two towering pine trees. It was a low-laying rectangular shack with wood paneling and a sloppy thatched roof. A fence made of twisted branches cordoned off a modest front yard, every square inch of which was packed with a dazzling array of flowers, save for a thin dirt path leading to a particle board door that had ballooned from the rain. The garden looked like a rumpled up green carpet bursting with pops of yellow, purple, red, orange, and white.

He unlocked the door and led her inside. The walls were concealed entirely by the spines of hundreds of books in varying size and color. They rested upon scrap metal shelves deliberately organized to maximize the wall space for more books. A square metal table sat in the center of the room, and under it, three transparent jugs of water and two large clay pots. On the right side of the hut, a fireplace nurtured a handful of fading coals.

"Have a seat," he said, gesturing to a stool by the door. He took off his converter and smiled, revealing a mouth of yellow but somehow still bright teeth, and he pointed to a hole in the hut's ceiling that housed a circuit board and a pair of palm-sized oscillating fans.

"Converter-safe," he said.

"Converter-safe?"

"That's a converter up there. You can take yours off in here. The walls and the door are insulated."

"Really?"

"Really."

"I think I'll keep mine on just to be safe."

"Suit yourself," he said, shuffling to the fireplace. "You hungry?"

"I've got my own food. Thanks. Can I offer you anything for the oil?"

"Honestly, a little company would be nice. I don't get to see people much."

The woman stood up. The hour of the day was indiscernible in this window-less, crack-less hut. "I could use a safe place to work on the bike. How about I wheel it up here and spend some time fixing it? We can talk if you'd like."

"Okay. I'd like that."

When she left the hut, a sherbet-colored evening sky swirled behind the ever-present black disks. She rolled the bike through grasses of various rigidities, over hills of arid terrain. She stashed it under a pine tree a short distance from the hut, slung the satchel over her shoulder and gathered her seed mix, water bottle, and purple pouch.

That night, laying on the cold ground in her fold-up next to the bike, she held the purple pouch in her hands, feeling the objects inside not only with her hands but with every ounce of her heart. She picked up her pipe for a moment before deciding against it. The ships did not howl.

All morning and afternoon the next day, the woman worked on the bike. She rebuilt the radiator, fashioned a new seat from a piece of scrap metal Elijah gave her, and wiped as much corrosion off the relay and the battery terminals as she could. Just after changing the oil, he called out to her from his hut.

"Care for a drink?" he said, donning a label-less bottle of brown liquid.

She wiped her greasy hands on her pants and met him inside. There, she sat on her same stool by the door as he poured the liquor into a blue coffee mug and a white plastic cup. He handed her the coffee mug. She took off her converter.

"So, what's it like being a messenger?" he said.

"I don't know. Hard."

"Well, everything's hard."

She took a sip and pursed her lips as the liquid fire rolled down her esophagus.

"When's the last time you had a drink?"

She shook her head. "Too long."

"Don't you get lonely being a messenger?"

"If I was lonely, I'd join a comm. Don't you get lonely living here?"

"Well, sure."

"Why don't you join a comm?"

He took a sip and curled his bottom lip into his mouth. "I don't think I'd do very well in one."

The woman took another sip.

"Those your tags?" he said, pointing to her neck.

"Mine and my husband's."

"I feared they might be. I'm sorry."

"Yeah."

"What about your kids? When'd you lose them? During the war or after?"

She jerked her elbows up from her knees and glared at him. "Who says I lost my kids?"

Elijah's eyes glistened in the firelight. His smile morphed the tops of his cheeks into jolly red balls. They stared at each other for a long time. She looked down at her mug.

"After," she whispered.

He pulled his lips together in a tight, solemn line and nodded softly. "I'm sorry about that. Really, I am."

The woman shook her head.

"You've never talked it through with anyone, have you?"

"No, and I'm sorry, but I'm not going to tonight."

"That's fine. That's fine. I understand. I won't pretend to know your pain. Got enough of that here to go around."

She took another sip.

"I lost him after, too. That guy in the picture."

"I'm sorry."

He shrugged. "Something changed in him when the war started. Did you notice how some people changed? Like they had given up already? He didn't wanna fight. Didn't wanna do anything. Sorta just resigned himself to it. We only survived because I begged him to leave the city. They'd torn it all down, and we hadn't figured the CO_2 thing out yet. We raided a convenience store before anyone else got to it. That was his idea."

Elijah rose from his chair and shuffled over to the fire. He put his hands over the sharp orange flames and closed his eyes. "We tried a comm. Well, I did, at least. He just didn't try anything. He couldn't. After about a year, he stopped talking. I knew it was only a matter of time at that point, so I built us this place. I wanted to be with him every single second I still could. I wanted to hold on to whatever he was still willing to give me, and I didn't want anyone or anything else in the world around us. Just a place where we could live out our days with our books and our flowers. One day he stopped eating, and I knew he'd be gone soon. I'd stay up at night just staring at him sleeping because I knew I'd never see him again. I knew I'd spend what godforsaken time I had left just begging for one more minute. Just one more. There wasn't enough to make him want to stay. I wasn't enough to make him want to stay."

He turned to the woman. His eyes raged, his mouth hung open, and his still rosy cheeks shone with the dampness of tears and the flickers of firelight. "That's all I want. One more minute. If I—," his voice cracked as he heaved through a sob. "If I just had one more minute with him, I could tell him so much that I didn't know then. God almighty just sixty seconds. I could get so much off my chest. I'd tell him I love him, and I'd kiss him and I'd hold him. I'd laugh with him. I'd look into his eyes. I'd see him. I'd see him again."

The woman put down her mug and walked towards her host. She knelt before him and took his shaking hands in hers. She looked at them. She held them while he wept, and then for some time after as the fire faded into ashes. Outside, the howling of the disks reverberated through the night.

The sound of crashing metal jolted the woman awake. Another crash, then a murderous scream, another crash. Blind in the darkness and trapped in the tent, the woman's steady hands belied the chaos around her, unzipping the vestibule in total silence.

Outside, the light of a paling moon cast sickle-shaped streaks of its reflection off two exoskeletal behemoths battering the side of Elijah's hut. A burst of warm light from inside penetrated the indigo night as one of them peeled back a section of ceiling with a terrible claw derived from some interplanetary gene pool of hell. The other one climbed straight up a wall and fell inside. Elijah screamed, and all manner of heinous noises spewed forth into the night. The two invaders croaked and slurped and screeched and ripped and crunched.

Revolver in hand, the woman bolted into the resin-scented darkness. She ran through the forest over a bed of pine needles and crouched behind a tree trunk out of earshot, but still in sight of the decimated hut. The night was calm for a moment before the invaders subjected the building to absolute carnage. They smashed its walls, tossed its contents, spilled its liquids. Another wall collapsed, then another, and as if the structure itself was bleeding, waves of books deluged to the ground. Even Elijah's dripping limbs — already stripped to the bone — flew up from the wreckage like tasseled batons, ready to be caught by the bed of death they manifested from.

A rapid series of mechanical clicks, like pill capsules rattling in a nearly empty bottle, emanated from just a few feet behind her. In a single, split-second motion, she spun around, unholstered the revolver, and fired one of its six rounds straight out in front of her. The shot made a glassy sound, as if bouncing off something at close range, and a third invader standing right beside her peeled back the four flaps of its mouth and released a cry so deafening it broke the web of saliva over its throat. It stood towering over her, armored and creedless, a maroon-colored colossus of limbs and claws, an alien agent of death driven as much by the conquest of this one woman in the forest as it was of an entire civilization.

It swiped at her, whisking its wild hand audibly through the air, but she ducked, and the claw smashed into the great meat of the tree. The tree shook and splintered after another calamitous slam. The invader's next swipe cut clear through the middle of the tree, and after a series of wooden moans, its leafy half thundered to the ground. As if spring loaded, the woman leapt out from behind the shattered trunk and fired two shots directly into the invader's salivating mouth. The monster reared back, limbs flailing, before lunging forth in a rage somehow even more palpable and acute. It swiped at her with mechanical speed, and although the woman fell far enough back to escape an instant death, she did not evade the single dagger-like claw that ripped through the leather of her pants and seared her quad. She stood tall and fired two more shots directly into her assailant's mouth. It reared backward, bellowed in animalistic fury, and raged away into the darkness. She fired her last shot into the cloud of leaves it left in its wake.

All three of the invaders were gone, and although the night appeared still, the ground, the rubble, and the trees still shuddered from the havoc that had befallen them. The woman collapsed to the ground with her legs straight out and her back against the trunk of the broken tree. Wincing, she pressed her left palm over her wound. Streams of blood — black and shiny in the night — gushed over her fingers. With a deep breath, she took her hand away and peeled off her shirt, and she managed to tie it down over the wound enough to slow the bleeding.

She sat there bleeding and breathing through her converter until dawnlight tickled the treetops and songbirds coaxed the forest from its slumber. After gazing warily at two disks Venn-diagramed in the morning sky, she summoned the strength to rise and limp to the hut.

Shards of wood and scrap metal littered the ground in every direction. One and a half walls still stood: the fireplace wall, including its miraculously intact chimney, and half of the front wall. Scores of books and brittle shards of the hut's construction lay strewn throughout the flower garden, smashing the petals into bleeding patterns. The fence was completely gone. Tables, chairs, and anything meant to be standing had been overturned or smashed. And all that remained of Elijah were bony red splinters scattered throughout the ashes, mixed in like common trash, as if the very purpose of their conception was to erode in this place.

She sifted through a pile of dusty clothes and plucked out the cleanest thing she could find. Ripping it into three long strips, she made a proper tourniquet for the wound and wrapped the rest of it over the leg, replacing her thoroughly blood-soaked shirt.

The painful midday hours were spent unthreading remnants of Elijah's tunic and whittling a short needle out of the end of a wire coat hanger. Before starting, she forced a handful of Elijah's jerky and a bottle of water down her throat. Then she made a fire and grabbed the brown liquor. She took a long swig, held the needle over the fire, and dumped the rest of the bottle straight into the wound.

All day she stitched and stoked the fire, breathing through her converter, not making sounds, and by the time she finished, another night had fallen. She removed the stool from under her and laid on the ground in its place. She was so cold she thought she might die, and there were moments during the first night when she wanted to.

For two more days, the woman stayed there and tended to the wound and nourished her body back to health with what sundries Elijah had left. When she finally was strong enough to stand, she redressed the wound and limped to the bike.

Pinned under a rock by the front tire was a handwritten note and a broken circuit board.

Thanks for listening.

- Elijah

She wheeled the bike over to the hut and filled its tank with fuel from a barrel behind the ruins. The last thing she saw on her way to the road was a picture frame with cracked glass, holding a photo of two happy men from a bygone era. She took the photo out of the frame and stuffed it into her purple pouch, not looking at the pouch's other contents.

Like a branch floating on a rushing river, the road wrapped the woman in its embrace and carried her off to wherever they both were going. They flowed together through trees and shrubs and acres of golden grain, through chill-toned winds and circling skies towards the message board and the asphalt road. Thunder rumbled softly above, and far out on the prairie, the woman saw herself on the front porch of a house. Next to her was a man in military fatigues. Running past a row of blazing red azaleas were two young children, one boy and one girl, and the woman held an infant in her arms. They were there and then they weren't, and then they were there again, and the front tire hit a loose rock and she launched headfirst over the handlebars. She clattered to the ground with a grunt and rolled like a rag doll through the grass and the rocky terrain.

The scrap metal seat she'd fashioned for herself had fallen off and the items in the saddlebag it held in place were scattered all over the dirt road. She had eyes only for the purple pouch. When she saw it in a pool of seed mix and silvery bike tools, she sprinted towards it, fell to her knees, and dumped it all out on the road.

Seeing those items sent a white-hot dagger of apoplectic rage through her lungs and her throat. Two pink hair barrettes, a small pair of green eyeglasses, an action figure, a dog collar, a wedding ring. A picture of two men embracing in paradise. She had nothing to remember the baby. The hate and the sorrow and the futility of it all rocketed through her entire body, and she crumbled into a heap of tears in the dirt. She screamed through her converter and beat the ground with her fists over and over and over again. No one heard her, save the wheatgrass dancing in the pre-storm wind.

Another groan of thunder rumbled through the hills. She rose, gathered her belongings, dusted off the bike, and rode north. The road she took was a familiar one. It was a road hammered out of brittle earth and dreams deferred. She churned through it, demanding passage, and grinding into it her imperative.

Up ahead, the sky had turned nearly as dark as the disks, and the two boulders propping up the message board poked through the curve of the earth.

PART 2

EL DIABLO

Some months later, a fire burned brightly in the blue desert night. The flames flickered back and forth in the darkness, as if enchanted, and the embers, bold in their brief moments of life, pulsated in the dry and popping heat. Gaff stared up at the stars — thousands of them — spinning and burning a million light-years away.

From the opposite side of the fire, the woman sat with her knees tucked into her chest and her back wedged against the flat end of a boulder. She puffed her pipe and eyed Gaff through a tower of rolling smoke.

They sat there like beings of an ancient age, solemn in the vastness of their surroundings, cloistered in the shadow of some old and fabled culture.

"We become them. I'm convinced of that," Gaff said after a long while. The dog tags around his neck flickered in the moonlight, as if it were them that spoke instead of him. There was something exotic in his voice and in his eyes.

A disk positioned far off in the north howled over the tranquil cracks of the fire. Gaff looked at it.

"You ever work with those guys from the 24th STS? What'd they used to call 'em?"

"Task Force White."

"Ah, yes. Task Force White. Crazy motherfuckers." He lifted his converter, flicked open a lighter, and lit a hand-rolled cigarette. "I met this guy right after the fall who said he jumped with them. Said he was part of a boarding unit that went inside. He went on for hours about the crew, the mission, his C.O. who ripped out right before things got gnarly. You would have hated this guy, a real kinda show-off type, a real blade runner."

She scoffed.

"He said the aliens inside the disks were not like the ones on the ground. Kept calling them 'smooth robots'. I guess some of 'em were, like, I dunno, melded to their machines. And they were all white. Imagine seeing a room full of these pale robotic things stuck in the walls, or merged into the floors, or there's arms bulging out of a computer terminal. Shit like that, he said, that he couldn't tell the difference between organic and machine. Said he just couldn't get over the insensitivity of it all. The coldness."

He shook his head and flicked ash onto the fire. Like many who had survived this long, Gaff's age was a relative mystery. This new world had hardened the young to become old and sharpened the old to become young. Those that couldn't meet in the middle perished or were discarded.

"This guy got me thinking. You gotta assume that if our species lasts long enough, we're probably headed that way, too. Or, if the invaders don't leave, and—"

"They're not leaving. I've heard people say that and they're wrong. They're not leaving."

Gaff leered at her. "My point is, it doesn't matter. Don't you see?"

"So then, why are we doing this?"

"Doing what?"

She gestured to their motorcycles, then to the fire, then to the desert. "This."

Gaff stood and looked long out over the blue caldera. The land out there was cold, arid, a broad and breathless stage upon which the only players were flakes of dust dancing on moonbeams. It had an almost sinister glow, the horizon of some icy and distant planet. There was nothing out there. Nothing at all.

The woman took another drag, pursing her lips tight and closing her eyes.

Gaff shivered. "Does that bitter grass stuff help you?"

"I don't know. I'm not really sure."

"Hmm. I've only ever had one dream. It's the same thing over and over."

"What is it?"

"It's not very pleasant."

"That's okay. I get it."

"Not this one, you don't." Gaff sat back down. He tossed a twig onto the fire and watched it wither away hissing.

"Something... something bad happened to me as a kid." He glared at her. "Do you know what I mean by that?"

"Think I have a pretty good idea."

"I was lying there wishing like anything for him to stop. I prayed to God, to the Devil. Anything. I wasn't even finished praying when my eyes were drawn to the corner of the classroom. It was the second grade classroom. I couldn't see anything, but I could feel another presence was there. It was a strong presence, watching. I felt it asking me something, or maybe asking my permission. More of a feeling than a question. I was so scared already, of course I said yes."

He took a heavy drag, blowing the smoke through his converter and into the fire.

"And right at that moment, my teacher dropped to the floor. I turned around, and he was dead. A heart attack! Right then and there. His eyes and mouth were stretched open so wide it looked like he had seen El Diablo himself, like he was stuck screaming in terror."

"That's a terrible dream."

He cackled. "That's no dream. That's my life. The dream came that night."

Another disk howled, this time from the west, and the one over to the north responded with a high, looping wail. Gaff hung his head.

"Have you ever had a dream that felt more real than a dream? That's what this felt like. It was so real. I was right there. I was back in that classroom, standing at a window that overlooked a great field behind the school. Way, way out in the field, I saw this... thing, like a little black speck way out there. It was very far away, but I could somehow tell it was there because of me, whatever it was. It was the same feeling I had when I felt that strong presence in the classroom. Only this time I could see it, and it was moving slowly towards me."

Gaff shifted uncomfortably, lowered his voice. The woman didn't move.

"I knew right there, right there in that first dream, that thing wanted something from me, and it wasn't gonna let me go until it got its way. It wasn't like an evil or a scary feeling, just very... I don't know, awkward. Almost shameful. The jealousy from this thing was so intense I felt ashamed. It wanted something from me badder than I've ever wanted anything in my life, badder than for my teacher to stop. It was still just a speck out there in the field when the dream ended. But the next night, I had the same dream, and the speck was a tiny bit closer and a tiny bit larger. Night after that? Same thing. The field, the speck, the awkward feeling, my eyes unable to look away. A little closer. A little closer."

He shook his head.

"I don't have this dream every day now, but it's still coming closer. Just a few steps at a time. The closer it gets, the more I can feel its desire, its hunger. Oh, does it hunger."

Gaff's voice became frail. Something about him seemed to falter, to retreat within himself. He did not look at the woman.

"It met me as a boy in that classroom and that's how it will always see me. It's very close to me now. I can see it clearly. It... it's dark. So dark. Something somehow blacker than black. It's not even a color. It's a stain. It's close to me. It's very close to me, you must understand. No matter what I do, I'm never going to get out of that classroom. I can't get out and it's coming for me. It's coming for me and it's almost here." He looked up at her and whispered. "I can see its face."

The woman's voice was equally soft. "What does its face look like?"

Gaff sighed. After a while, he said, "I don't want to say that part out loud."

The woman put her pipe away and pulled her sleeping bag over her legs. "What do you think it is? What do you think it means?"

Gaff turned back to the fire. Its dying light cast a shimmering reflection across his face. "I don't know what it is but I think I know what it means. Some kind of countdown. Closer and closer." He pointed to her pipe. "So, you could imagine what that dream weed might do to me."

"I don't dream of demons. I dream of angels."

Gaff let out a chuckle that collapsed into a hacking cough.

Three birds of prey flapping high across a rocky escarpment drew their attention away. The woman tracked them with her eyes as they banked around the talus slope and evaporated into the night. "I think I believe there's something inside them," she said.

"Inside what?"

"Dreams."

"What's inside them?

"Answers. It sounds like you'll get yours soon." She looked at him and rose. "I'm bedding down."

Gaff did not look at her, did not respond. He sat transfixed on the dying fire, alone there in the darkness, almost in a stupor, watching the coals blacken until they could black no more.

An uneasy feeling came over the woman as she zipped closed the fold-up and laid down. The purple pouch sat in the corner of the tent, but she didn't retrieve it.

When sleep took her, she found herself staring up at a massive pair of legs swinging high above. Their host was seated on a piano bench — her piano bench — and the legs were her daughter's. The song coming from the piano was something of a dirge, a wretched harmony both warped and pulverizing. The legs descended a staircase into a murky and unlit chamber. On the back wall, the woman's daughter, naked, was hanging Christ-like in shackles. The girl's body had been crudely severed from the waist-down, gobs of blood dripping and entrails dangling where legs should have been. The wall receded, but the bisected child remained, and behind her, the background morphed into a fiery hellscape of scorched and ruined land. Her daughter lifted her head so that her eyes were level with the horizon, and when she opened her mouth to speak—

The screech of a passing hawk startled the woman awake, and the light of a crystal blue morning raked at her eyes. She sat up and shot a rueful glance at the purple pouch, as if it had been somehow lost in a dream and was now miraculously recovered. She took a deep breath, rubbed her eyes, and stepped outside.

Gaff was already gone, not leaving behind a scrap of physical evidence. Even the footprint of his tent had been brushed or windswept, such that the blades of hard desert grass had already regained their shape.

The woman's knees popped as she walked stiff and stilted to her bike, the flesh of her mostly healed leg wound throbbing. She peeled off her leather jacket under the heat of a sun blazing high in the eastern sky.

The bike's seat cover, still just the lockless scrap metal from Elijah's, lay bent on the ground by the bike.

"What the fuck?" she said, peering into an empty saddlebag.

Everything was gone: revolver, bullets, binoculars, tools, med kit, food, water, flashlight, fire tools, new helmet, all her spare clothes. Even the satchel that would have held essentials for an outland trek.

"You mother—," she glanced down at the fuel tank, bone white and empty. "Fuck! You motherfucker!"

She slammed her fists down on the chassis and screamed into the sky. She kicked fruitlessly at the dust and screamed again, and she ran out to the road in an apoplectic fury. The road — like her saddlebags, like the desert — was utterly void.

"I'm gonna kill you," she said, marching back to her fold-up with balled fists, "I'm gonna fucking kill you!"

She clawed back the tent flap and took stock of what she still had: sleeping bag, pipe, lighter, purple pouch. Then she picked up the entire tent by its poles and launched it headlong over a boulder. It clattered against the warm and unforgiving caliche.

The route that had led to this place was an old service road far off the trail of any traveler who might use this godforsaken place for passage. It would take the better part of a week to reach the highway on foot.

The woman sat on the boulder and gazed bare eyed in the opposite direction of the service road, scanning the horizon for some guidance in that emptiness. Out there was a vast and dry caldera, its cracked mosaic floor forged out of eons-old lava. Past the rim and slopes of ash-flow tuff around it, copper mesas jig-sawed the azure horizon like the skyline of a volcanic metropolis. The bend of a river looped around a mesa at the edge of the firmament, and some miles south beyond that, another road.

"Fuck," she said, squinting at the river and that southern road.

The noonday sun was directly above her. She closed her left eye, positioned one hand against the sun, and tipped her index finger clockwise until it landed on the western disk.

"Three and a half hours. Maybe four."

Back at the boulder, she dusted off the tent and placed it back upright. She retrieved the bike and the bent metal seat and laid them both down beside the tent. Before crawling inside, she draped her unzipped sleeping bag and her jacket over the vestibule to block the sun.

"I hope the Devil does fucking take you," she whispered. "I'll give you your El Diablo. She's coming, alright."

For the next three and a half hours, the woman sat closed eyed and cross-legged in the tent, resting her mind as much as her body. When at last the sky began to redden and the sun was half-eclipsed behind the western disk, she wrapped her sleeping bag, her bike seat, a few dead coals, and her purple pouch in the lining of the tent, lashed the lining to her back with string from the poles, draped her jacket over her head, and struck out towards the river.

She marched with a posture and a purpose that was corporal to her being, a muscle memory inscribed multiple lifetimes ago. They said back then that she might one day be a general, that she had the constitution to lead. For a fleeting moment, she recalled the goodness of those days as a late afternoon alpenglow dripped down the cut of the mountains.

The red evening saw her through the terra-cotta landscape like some fanatical archeologist, driven so madly into the rocky wilderness she cursed survival by sheer presence in this place. Rows of cacti danced on land around her, a half-set sun casting their shadows long into the valley like the spears of goblins.

By the time the woman crossed the caldera, the shadows had melted, and the light of an unrisen moon dyed the world a cool blue, and all the rugged and serrated land looked once again dead from one axis to the other. The throbbing in her leg had been worsening for hours, and the tens of thousands of steps behind her burned like hell in her boots. Yet those maladies paled in comparison to the wicked thirst baking in her throat. It got so bad that by nightfall she took out her converter to better retain any speck of moisture that might be floating through the dead and arid air.

She went on as far as she could that night, as far as anyone could, until at last the distance and the thirst and the pain forced her down. The river was still miles away.

"Goddammit," she said. "Goddammit all."

There was nothing special about where she landed — no structure or shelter — just more of the same wasteland that lay ahead, behind, and in every other direction. She didn't even take off her boots or build the tent, she just put her jacket on and laid down and tried to forget about the world. After a few minutes of washing pockets of saliva around in her mouth, she fell asleep.

A few hours later, she woke to a pale orange sun cradled in the canyon. She cleared her bone-dry throat and tried coaxing up saliva, only to choke on epiglottal cobwebs spun the day before. Blood had begun seeping through the area of her pants covering the wound, and upon noticing, she opened her mouth to curse, but nothing came out. Instead, she massaged the searing muscle while gazing forward at the volcanic headland. It was dawn quiet out there. Not a sign of life or scrap of wind.

A moment of panic ensued when she realized she'd slept without her converter. She scrambled to put it back in and check the bars. When only four of the six lit up, she got moving again.

The river was in sight now and the mesas were closer, and as the sun rose and the heat built, sprigs of green and black weeds appeared more abundantly beneath her aching feet. What began as a tranquil murmur in the distance sharpened into a series of gushes, trickles, tumbles, and plops.

"El Diablo," the woman whispered to herself, smiling, "Can't kill the devil that easy."

Her knees nearly gave out when she finally reached the bank. She threw off her makeshift pack, stripped her clothes, peeled off boots, and waded in. The water wasn't cold, yet soothed bones and blistered feet within seconds of entering. She took a mouthful, swished it around, spat it out. Inch by inch, she slid forward on knees, soaking shoulders, jaw, eyes, the tip of head. She released a great exhale underwater, bubbles clouding her view and tickling her face.

Later, she strode back to shore, retrieved her pack, and walked it over head to the other bank. She unfurled its contents in the mesa's shadow, first setting the purple pouch on a rock well away from the water.

She ripped off the tent's vestibule with her teeth, bent the metal bike seat into a sort of pot shape with her hands, placed the coals in a dugout she clawed into the dirt, and lit the coals with the lighter. Only after much negotiation did they spark, and as handfuls of picked weeds fed a small fire, she constructed a lean-to style frame with the tent poles, lined the well of the pot with detached vestibule, filled the pot with river water, and set it atop of the frame.

Two magpies glided down from the mesa and landed on the opposite riverbank. The woman froze, and not taking her eyes off the birds, found a pebble in the silt and beamed it at them. It struck nowhere close, and the magpies flapped off. She cursed and went back to work.

Once the water was boiling, she took the pot off the frame and leaned over it and cooled it to a lukewarm temperature with pointed breath. Her depleted arms shook as she raised the pot to her lips and drank. Still hot water crashed through her mouth and down her throat. When the pot was almost empty, she tilted it and poured the rest of the water in, streams of it lapping down her cheeks.

She boiled enough water to drink a few cupfuls each day and clean out her wound. After a few days, she'd even found middling success as an angler, constructing a trap out of the vestibule and the tent poles. The best spot wasn't at the river bend where she assumed it would be, but about a hundred yards further downstream where the banks narrowed and the current eddied around the hull of a half-submerged motorboat.

On the fourth day, as she made her way back to camp, a sharp point of light caught her eye amidst the evening rays shimmering off the pan. Something old and shiny and circular was lodged into the indiscriminate desert vermillion. She scrambled over to the spot and found an old metal coffee can, clear and gleaming as if someone had simply put it there. She grasped it in both hands, cried out in joy, and nearly wept.

That night, she boiled three full cans of water and drank every last drop.

More than a week had passed by the time she left for the southern road, striking out at dusk over the moonlit caldera. The indentations of her boots sat crystalized in the icy blue dirt, a moonwalker's path.

A cloud of bats coughed forth from a distant cave and wafted high above. They knifed through the night air, squeaking in some secret code, and then they dissipated westward. Two days ago, the disk patrolling that spot had floated upward and vanished into the predawn haze.

The woman stopped only once that night to sip water and eat a single grilled fish, one of six she'd wrapped up in the tent vestibule. She'd filled the coffee can to the brim and slung it to her shoulder with a tent pole string, and she jury-rigged the old bike seat into a lid that mostly worked. The sun hung low into the next day, a day the woman spent resting and waiting and thinking in the shelter of the tent. She smoked her pipe and slept through the afternoon, and it was there that she saw him again.

He looked the same in every dream, the size of a giant, a celestial pillar of strength in his dress blues. He was always alone, always outside, always so far away. The disks were never there, they wouldn't dream of it. They wouldn't dare. She ran towards him. Her husband lumbered through the folds of the mountains as if passing messages between them. He was walking away from her. She was too small for him to see. She ran faster. She called out to him. She ran faster. She ran harder. She screamed his name into the clouds, catapulting empty hopes they might alert him. They did not, and he did not hear her. He did not see her. He did not know she was there. The void chasm between them turned into a shackle on her heart. It pressed on her shoulders and broke her back. It pushed her down, down, down—

She woke with a strangling pain in her chest, as if a part of her had been hollowed out. She coughed and winced and seethed through clenched teeth, groaned as the pain churned inside her. Rigid fingers clutched her shirt as the pain intensified, scorching her, swimming towards the one right spot in her heart.

She sat there rocking back and forth and crying, magpies picking peacefully at the shrubs outside what was left of the tent.

When finally the pain decided she'd had enough, it released its grip and returned to its latent slumber, lying in wait to resurface the next time all she had lost became real again.

But pain would not deter her from them. Nothing would.

Heaven that night poured all of its stars onto a glittering obsidian canvas. Red balls of light other worlds — blinked at her through the tail of the lion, the belt of the hunter, the horns of the bull. Lucent beams from the Milky Way split the night into diagonal halves: one end sinking behind the pale placard hills, the other arching up and bleeding out into some ether of the cosmos.

Every now and then, those very stars would coax her eyes up from the desert floor. They were the compass, the waypoints lighting her path to the road, mapping the world in a way invaders couldn't ruin. And yet, even in moments when her direction was determined, her gaze and her heart would there linger, peering through sections of the sky like windows to memories that felt like home. They summoned fond ruminations of different days and different times because they, unlike everything down here, remained unchanged. While thinking about him again, she said, "I miss you so much."

In this place, the woman was alone, but she kept moving and gazing. Even as the throbbing in her legs crescendoed, as if voodoo-bound to the newly rising sun, she marched on until at last the southern road drew within sight.

A kettle of vultures drifted yonder like specks of dirt circling a drain. One of them fell lifeless through the air, and the crack of a gunshot some great distance away came a few seconds later. Another vulture was shot, then another, then one after the other until all were downed.

The woman pitched the tent on the side of the road and sat inside, waiting. After only an hour, the hum of a motor rose to the east. It was an old white minivan mounted with off-road tires and piled with bags strapped to the roof. It drove slowly, almost lumbering, seemingly as curious about the bedraggled hitchhiker it had encountered as she was about it. The woman raced out to the middle of the road and waved her arms. The van pulled over.

"What do you want?" said the driver, an elderly mustached man with dark sunglasses. A younger man with a machine gun sat in the passenger seat, and several sets of timid eyes from the back curled around the window sills to consider the woman.

"I need passage to the next comm. I'll go wherever you're going. I… I've been out here alone and I'm almost out of water."

He lowered his sunglasses. "You're alone? What happened to you?"

"I got lost."

"Lost?"

She didn't answer.

He leered at her. "If this is some kinda jackpot, Ernie will shoot you on sight," he said, throwing a backward thumb over his shoulder towards the unmoving passenger.

"It's not. Look at me. All I have is my tent."

He looked at the tent, a ripped and dusty mess, then back at her. "What can you pay for a ride? The folks back there paid a lot."

"I don't have a thing to my name that I can give you."

He shook his head. "How'd you say you got here again?"

Ernie leaned forward and whispered something into the driver's ear.

The woman stared at them both. "Listen. Tie me up and put the gun on me the whole time. I don't care. I'm starving and thirsty and I just need to get—"

"I say again, what can you pay?"

She took a step back and examined each of the faces in the back. Two adults, two teenagers, two children. All of their converters looked exactly the same. "Where are you taking these people?"

The driver scoffed and started the engine.

"Wait! I'm a messenger. I'll deliver three messages for you anywhere on the western flank for free."

"Really?"

"Yes. For free. Please. I can help you if you help me. Just get me to the next comm, that's all I ask. I'll be quiet. I'll be... just, please."

He looked at Ernie, and Ernie nodded.

"Ok, drop your bag there and get in. Ernie's gonna search it."

"Can I stand here while he searches?"

"No. Get in."

Ernie and the woman passed each other in front of the vehicle. He stopped her with a stiff palm to the shoulder.

"Gotta search you first," he said. Ernie was a large man, strong but unchiseled, his presence hard and severe. His dark eyes, hollow like gun bores, stabbed the woman with a penetrating clarity.

He patted her down, then opened the tent and squeezed his frame inside. His back to the woman, he rifled through the contents but stopped, closely examining something.

"Let's go!" yelled the driver through a dingy converter.

Ernie emerged from the tent. "You better hold on to this," he said, handing her the purple pouch. "The rest of that shit stays. We don't have time to pack it. This road is monitored."

The woman tucked the pouch into her pants and got into the van. She sat in the first backseat row next to a middle-aged woman. Long hair, dull skin, maybe forty.

"My name's Olifia," she said, shuffling through a backpack at her feet.

The woman nodded curtly.

"Here." Olifia placed two apples and a bottle of water in the woman's lap.

The woman recoiled. "Are you serious?"

"You said you were starving, right? Eat up."

She gaped at the apples for a few seconds before tearing into one. "Oh my God," she said between ravenous bites. "Thank you. Thank you for this."

All were quiet for a while after the woman ate her apples and drank her water. The shamelessness she displayed in devouring her gifts did something to dissipate the tension of her unceremonious arrival.

"We're headed to 226," Olifia said. "Just in case you were wondering."

The woman examined each of the faces behind her before responding. A man of roughly Olifia's age, a teenage boy, a teenage girl, and two young girls on either side of the man, one blonde and one brunette.

"You guys all family?" said the woman.

Olifia pointed at the teenagers. "That's my son Pin, my daughter Sarnia. Back there with our two twin girls is my husband, Jackson."

"Nice to meet you," Jackson said.

"You're traveling alone?" Olifia said.

"Yeah," said the woman.

"Well, I've got a good feeling about you. You can be a part of our crew until we part ways."

The woman chuckled. "I appreciate that. And I really appreciate the food."

"You said you're a messenger?"

"When I'm not out starving in the desert, yes."

"That must be interesting."

"I suppose so."

"Well, I think what you do is a wonderful thing for humanity. It's so important to keep us all connected as we rebuild. I know it's not easy." She paused for a while and then continued. "You get to enjoy the open road. The landscape is beautiful. Even the ugly parts aren't ugly anymore, wouldn't you agree? I think it may even be more beautiful than it used to be. I think—"

Jackson put a hand on Olifia's shoulder.

"Sorry. I'm sorry," Olifia said. "I go on like that sometimes."

"All good," said the woman. "We need more people with your attitude. I could learn something from it."

Ernie twisted his head around to examine the woman. His eyes lingered on hers for a long moment, as if assessing their depth or asking a silent question.

"Camp's about an hour away," said the driver. "I'll take first watch, Ernie'll take second. I'm gonna want to be back on the road by dawn. If we stay on schedule, we'll be at the 226 around noon." He glanced at his passengers in the rearview mirror. "Sound okay?"

Everyone nodded.

"Okay on food? Water? How you doin' there, messenger?"

"I'm great. Thank you. Thanks to all of you."

"I'm Desmond, by the way. I don't think I got your name, did I?"

"No, you didn't," said the woman.

Desmond chuckled and gazed out at the receding light rimming the horizon.

The arid orange lands smoothed out into rocky and shrub-filled plains. They camped about ten miles off the road at sunset, obscured from travelers by a copse of conifers and a loping hill that slid down into a valley. Several old camp chairs and a recently used firepit waited for them.

The two younger girls got out of the van and scanned the edges of the valley, their high voices like the humming of bees under their converters. Ernie yanked open the van's back doors and began pulling out plastic crates and firewood. At one point, he dabbed an index finger on a dark red spot on one of the stones surrounding the fire pit. He sniffed the finger, then flicked away whatever residue had latched to him.

Desmond walked backwards and used his hands to talk as he led the party to the pit. "Now, I call this little spot Rainbow's End. Kid you not, I found it exactly in that manner. I took a little boy this same route a few years back, and he demanded — I mean really demanded — that we find the end of a rainbow hanging off the edge of that hill there. Can you believe it led us right here? So, I think this place has good luck for us."

That night, the group ate quickly and spoke quietly. The children verbalized their dreams of Comm 226, of games, of other children, of picking flowers in the rain. Desmond regaled the teenagers with tales of journeys past, of run-ins with bandits and escapes from invaders. Ernie said nothing, the woman said nothing.

After participating in the group conversation for a short while, Olifia got up from the fire and shut herself inside the van. Jackson followed and rocked her in his arms as she wept. Ernie checked on them, but Jackson assured him all was well, and by the time Ernie returned to the fire, night had fallen.

The woman couldn't sleep that night. When the dark was at its deepest, something compelled her to crawl out of the tent. Ernie sat there alone, stoking the scullery fire, twisting and examining the poker as if deriving some further meaning from its action. He said nothing to the woman as she sat bleary-eyed in the camp chair across from him. She jammed her balled fists into the chair's mesh cup holders. The fabric was white from weather and age.

"What really happened out there?" Ernie said, not looking at her.

"Huh?"

"Someone like you doesn't get lost. What happened?"

"If you're really dying to know, someone abandoned me."

"Who?"

"It doesn't matter."

"Yes, it does. Who?"

The woman sat up. "The hell's your problem?"

"I don't have a problem. I'm not out in the middle of the desert trusting people I just met."

"Who the hell are you, anyway?"

"Me? I'm nobody."

"Look at me."

He looked at her.

"I'm going to kill the motherfucker who did it. Trust me. I'm going to fucking murder him."

"Good," he said, turning back to the fire. He raised the hot end of the poker to his eyeline, wielding it like a saber. Charred bits of wood flaked from its tip, falling neon orbs of light that cascaded down into the darkness. "I hope you do."

The woman shook her head. She leaned back and began tracing constellations with her eyes. After fumbling with his tent zipper for a moment, Desmond stumbled out and relieved himself in plain view of them.

Ernie sighed. "Let me guess. Air Force?"

"How'd you know?"

"You have a rigidity."

She scoffed. "What about you?"

"I didn't serve."

"Really? You sure have an attitude."

He laughed at the comment. "I'm sorry. I'm trying to work on it."

"Work harder."

Ernie gazed up at the stars with her. "I was a graphic designer before this. Never touched a gun, never got in a fight."

"No shit?"

"No shit."

"That happens. Some of the biggest badasses I served with wilted when shit got real, and some of the ones we least expected stepped up."

"We all have our stories about the fall. I won't bore you with mine. Let's just say I'm not exactly proud of what I did."

"Had to do."

"Huh?"

"What you had to do. Not what you did. You did what you had to do."

"God will decide."

She shook her head.

He threw another log onto the fire, paused, and pointed up. "That one there's been following us."

The woman looked up over her shoulder at the disk beyond the canyon.

"Following you?"

"Yes."

"Not sure I've ever heard of a disk that follows."

"Maybe I'm just losing it." He leaned forward and squinted at it. "Sometimes—"

Ernie froze, jostled violently. The poker dropped from his open hand and clattered in time with the whelp of the bullet piercing his flesh. A thin, horizontal gush of blood sprang from his forehead, as if an artisan had drilled through his skull and turned on a tap in his brain. The second bullet whizzed over the woman's ear. It sent her scrambling under the meager cover of her camp chair, but the next shot zinged right through the meat of her left shoulder. In and out. She sprinted to the van through geysers of dirt stirred up by more gunshots erupting around her.

The first motorcycle came barreling over the crest of the hill bearing two men — maybe men — the driver grim and clad in black goggles and a leather skull cap strapped under his chin, eyes locked on the camp. His passenger, with shears of a torn and bloodstained sundress flapping madly behind him and a pair of antlers fixed to his head, kneeled on a board bolted to the chassis and held his finger all the way down on the trigger of a semi-automatic machine gun seemingly without mind for target, firing and firing and firing again, laughing and screaming over the devastating cracks of its violence.

What seemed like hundreds of them followed over every angle of the rim, crazed and swarming warriors carving through the darkness and staining the black night red. Some wore exotic military uniforms, gaudy jackets flared with ribbons of superfluous rank and trophies of the slain, their necks draped with lanyards of dried human ears and fingers and eyes, and flakes of bone and cartilage sawed from dead invaders. Some of their bodies were half or even fully naked, painted or outfitted with bright jewels and goggles and articles more befitting of a pageant than a slaughter. Most rode in on small engine motorcycles whose thunder echoed through the bowl as they advanced. Others careened brakeless down the flanks in vehicles as strange and mutilated as their drivers, twisted machines bearing all manner of lights and noise and some even music, some mounted with heavy tires and plates of armor and every type of gun, some dragging trailers ushering more men and more guns and empty dog cages and only devils may know what else.

Two of the main vehicles — both with the word MOTHERLESS

spray-stenciled on their sides — crashed right into each other next to the fire, crunching their armored frames together and driving off in maniacal fashion. Some of the bikers parked by the tents while others leapt like kamikazes into the air as their grinding metal steeds crashed into whatever or spun out aimless in the dirt.

The sheer noise they generated was a weapon itself: over-torqued engines, heinous battle cries, sadistic laughter, bellowing shotgun blasts, quick raps of pistol fire, thumping hums of machine guns. A teenage boy stepped out of one of the vans wearing a converter ending in a long hose that dangled at his waist like the trunk of an elephant, an umbrella in one hand and a sword in the other. He sliced open the top of the tent housing Olifia's children.

Pin lunged with flames in his eyes and tackled him to the ground. Nearly a dozen of them dove on top of the pair in a rabid flail, raining down a hailstorm of blows and coyote-like yelps onto both victim and assailant. Jackson emerged from the van with his hands in the air and began pleading, and a man painted purple wearing a headdress and a single boot — nothing else — walked up and shot him in the head. Olifia wailed as another one dragged her by the hair away, and like some melodramatic Renaissance fresco, four sets of hands — one from a mother, three from her daughters — grasped for each other in futility as humans harvested from the same primordial soup pulled them apart forever.

A giant of a man, shoulders back and gut forward, grabbed the two twin girls and carried them under each arm towards cages that had been thrown out of a trailer and set on the ground. He dropped them without caution, the skull of the brunette smacking the edge of the cage, and a group of men bound their limbs and threw them into the cages as they screamed and cried. Another man was having his way with the teenage girl, Sarnia. She lay expressionless, with her hands up by her head and tears streaming down the sides of her face. Pin was dead when they finally peeled him off the ground, his head lolling and his entire head and torso shimmering in crimson blood. The teenager with the sword and the umbrella was dead too, bludgeoned by his comrades in the bedlam of the pile. They threw both bodies into the back of a truck.

Not long after they were done with the family, the woman was located under the van and yanked out by the feet and thrown in a cage herself. Originally designed for a large dog, the cage limited the woman's bound arms and legs to only a few inches of mobility, and she seethed and shot her eyes wildly at the men poking and laughing at her. Someone tied a blindfold over her eyes.

"Take this one straight to the Crone," one of them said.

While Desmond leaned on the hood of the van and exchanged something with one of the marauders, he pointed to Ernie's bullet-riddled corpse still sitting in the camp chair, still gazing at the fire. "Meat's still good on that one, too."

An indeterminate amount of time saw the woman shipped and shackled and jostled and pulled out of the cage and put back in, yanked and prodded and picked at and laughed at, and finally bound to a wheelchair. When they removed the blindfold, her eyes were stained by the dim yellow ooze of halogen lights, rows of them bolted to a ceiling high above. It was a great hall, maybe an old gymnasium, vast and bare of any decoration.

Scores of Motherless, ranging in all shapes and genders, stood along the chamber's perimeter. They wore no clothing save for white briefs, and their matching white painted bodies would have been their most garish feature had their faces not been done up to look like mimes or jesters. Some even wore brightly colored cockscomb hats.

One of them wheeled the woman across the chamber's shimmering tile floor, the chair's axle squeaking in an odd rhythm against the barefoot plods of the pusher.

Something deep inside the woman repelled the urge to gaze upon the thing in the middle of the chamber, the thing she was being wheeled towards. Every eye in the place besides hers was on it, and even when it addressed her, the woman refused to look.

"Is this a lamb or a lion?" said the Crone, voice purely mechanical.

The woman didn't answer. No one did.

"There are pens for lambs and dens for lions. There are places they will go. Many, many utilities."

A creature of great corpulence, the Crone sat naked at a wooden table supported on both ends by waist-high file cabinets. The table's surface had been notched to accommodate her massive stomach, an ivory boulder parting the two drooping, triangular shaped breasts that served as the only hint of her gender. Her head was completely bald, and instead of a converter over her face, a surgically installed filtration machine was clamped onto and into her throat, orange lights winking. It was plugged into a machine by her side. One hand, a lifeless, club-like loaf, rested by a greasy keyboard attached to a speaker her fingers danced on to speak. The other, severed at the forearm and bearing some ghastly contraption, itched her massive, sloping side.

"You need not fear my lions. They are penitent." The monotone words spilled from her lips like acidic gruel. "They do not maim my lambs."

The pusher wrapped a hand around the woman's jaw and wrenched it up to force her to look at the Crone.

"Did they maim you, my lamb?"

"They shot me in the shoulder, if that's what you mean."

One of the Motherless strode forward bearing a platter of meat, cuts both thin and thick, one limb with the bone still in.

The Crone's gaze, as if magnetized, glommed onto the platter and tracked it closely, and the slight lean she made towards it released creaks from the reinforced bench upon which she sat. The Motherless placed it in front of her and she began eating, using her arm contraption to pick through the meat and shovel it into her mouth. She ate with a disturbing compulsion, shameless in her wanton gorging, chewing, and slurping. One might assume she had not eaten in days if not for the empty platters just like it scattered about the table and the floor.

"We do not hunger here. Do you hunger, my lamb?"

The woman recoiled.

Somehow, the Crone increased the pace of her eating, barely stopping between syllables to chew and swallow. She ate with her mouth mostly open, the pouch of flesh beneath her chin wobbling, the fingers of her other hand typing. "What is it that you hunger for?"

"Why am I here?"

"I can see into your heart, into your rawness. My lions tell me you are not like the others. Yet, you come to me lacking fortitude. Were they wrong about you?"

"I don't know what you're talking about. I'd like to leave. Is that an option?"

"You wish to deny my offer?"

The woman shot frantic glances at the many unmoving guards staring at them. "I'm not sure what you're offering me."

"A purpose."

"What do you want with me?"

"What are you?"

"What?"

The Crone stopped eating, the weight of her pause sucking the gravity out of the room. "You are a scared little girl."

"I'm a messenger."

"I have seen many like you. The lost ones. Telling yourself you have meaning, mourning your past. That's your purpose, isn't it? You subsist on the false relevance of their memory."

"I'd prefer it if you let me out of here. I don't want any part of what you're doing."

"We have a focus here that looks to the future. You're being offered a part."

"Get me the fuck out of—"

"I will not release you until I know what you are. It's information that will inform the manner in which you leave this room." The Crone turned in place just a few inches, as far as her mass was capable, but the gesture somehow signaled two more Motherless sentried on the wall to walk over to the pusher and escort him out of the chamber. The pusher began screaming, pleading. The Crone waited for the doors to close and the echoes of his panicked cries to subside before continuing. "And there are many manners in which you could leave this room."

The woman spoke softly with her head down. "I don't care. Hurt me. Do whatever you need to fit your bullshit creed. If you want to kill me, then go ahead with that. Maybe you'd be doing us both a favor. I will make a great meal. Just avoid my shoulder."

Another Motherless on the rear wall started laughing hysterically, a hyena at a funeral. None of the others reacted, and neither did the Crone. The guard just kept laughing.

"What the hell is happening here?" said the woman, shifting in the wheelchair.

The Crone grinned, teeth yellow and wild. With her eyes on the woman, she slammed the arm bearing her eating contraption onto the table's brittle wood, and she reached her typing hand across her incredible girth to unscrew it. She reached inside the file cabinet to retrieve another contraption, this one executing the mechanics of an ear tag applicator that might be used on livestock. But there was no livestock in this world.

"You would not make a good meal. Fear poisons the meat of a dying animal, and you are addled with fear. You are blind. Let me show you."

A new pusher began wheeling the woman towards the Crone. Before rounding the corner of the table, they passed a barrel containing electric cattle prods, band saws, sharpened poles, and other makeshift to be employed should the effects of the Crone's garish prosthetics be less severe. The woman slouched in the wheelchair. Something in her eyes and her face changed as she grew closer to this mostly human monstrosity. The guard in the back was still laughing. The Crone screwed the tagging contraption into her arm and wiped something off her face.

"Look into your heart, my lamb. I have. What is it that you fear? What poisons you? Not me, not these lions. Not even these invaders. What you fear is core to your being. I cannot evade it by killing you in your sleep. To nourish the bodies of those that will inherit the earth is a noble purpose, but we have no taste for poisoned meat."

The Crone didn't look at the woman as the wheelchair rounded the table. The tile under and around her was littered with stains and scraps of food. Directly under the bench, a bucket sat reeking of waste. A lone fly scuttled along its brim, crazed and ravenous for the manna produced above.

"When you wake up in the morning, does it take you a moment to recall what you've lost? Do you search your heart only to find them dead over and over again? Your greatest fear has become your reality." Something splashed into the bucket, and three more flies picking at the floor flew inside. "With each day that passes, do they move a little further away?"

The woman squirmed in the wheelchair.

"You need not walk this broken earth in guilt and fear. What took them away from you could not have been prevented. Even if you believe it was your fault, it was not your fault. What mother could have been expected to save her children from the annihilation of her species? No one. No mother."

"Don't you say another—"

"Hear me. Your life now is not a curse, no matter what you believe. It is a blessing. You must understand this. We are the lucky few who fell through the cracks of fate. Now, we must harness our luck. We must wield it. We cannot be afraid of the gift we have been given. Don't you understand? You, my lamb, you cannot be afraid of it."

The Crone sighed, and more objects plopped into the bucket. More flies followed.

"I see in you a raging fire. White hot it burns. Your guilt and your grief engulf you. All the little moments you remember, all the opportunities you chide yourself over missing. Let it all go. Let them all go. Take your fire and channel it into rebuilding this world with us. You have a useful set of skills, and we wish to use them. Consider this your invitation."

With incredible speed, the Crone wrapped her meaty typing hand around the back of the woman's head and yanked it to her bosom. The move seemed to shift the tone of the entire room, her bulk swaying and the bench creaking in agony. The Motherless were silent, almost reverent. The woman's curses were muffled by the Crone's flesh.

The Crone placed a pink tag over the woman's ear and bolted it through the helix using the contraption on her arm. The woman winced and jerked back but barely moved in the Crone's iron grasp. She shot daggers of rage into the Crone's foul, gray eyes from an upside-down headlock.

The Crone held her for a moment, looking at her, thinking about her, and then she released her and started eating and typing again. "Why did we lose this earth? Why were we not prepared?"

A faint trickle of blood pooled in the shell of the woman's ear and rolled down her cheek. The cartilage around the tag began to swell.

"Focus is what we strive for here. It is a powerful and overlooked tool. It is, in fact, the only tool. The fall reminded us of that. We had the means to conquer the invaders at our disposal, yet we did not execute. Why? Out of love for this so-called humanity. A humanity decimated and forgotten. What good did our compassion do us then?"

"Spare me this shit. I've heard it all before. There's no guarantee those weapons would've worked, even if we had used them."

"In order to survive, we must regain our focus. The new world demands it. We must cut ties with these bogus moral contracts. I, for one, question the judgment of their signatories. Did God sign them? Where is he? Did you sign them? Did your children?"

The woman heaved breaths in her wheelchair. She closed her eyes.

"Do not regard me with such disdain. I was a mother once, too. Every person on this earth has lost something they never dreamed of losing, even the children who came after the fall. They lost it before they were born. A raw deal, if you ask me."

The Crone shot her eyes up to the pusher and he snapped into action, wheeling the woman away.

"We will not sell our children out. When animals more powerful than us threaten our existence, we will not remain beholden to the supposed refinements of our evolution. We are rewriting the natural law because there isn't one anymore."

The pusher wheeled the woman backwards, ushered her out of the chamber, threw her into a cage bolted to the bed of a white pickup truck, and drove off.

The pickup passed through a commune defiled. Mountains of dog cages with human occupants, swarms of gun mounted vehicles, hundreds of Motherless yelling and fighting and raping and rewriting laws of their nature. An angled flagpole had been turned into gallows with three naked bodies twisting in the wind. The limbs had been cut off of all of them. The ground they rode on may have been grassy at one point, but now it was a dingy cocktail of mud and loose asphalt. Most of the windows of what appeared to be school buildings had been boarded up or busted out.

Sharpened timbers, like the pencils of giants, stood in a tightly packed wall around the compound's perimeter, and every one of them displayed some decrepit remnant of a conquered foe. Human heads, skulls, arms, legs, sometimes a whole body. Shriveled carcasses of invaders, many with open jaws wrapped around the timbers as if ready to consume them. Older stains of blood and entrails from these ornaments painted the top half of the wall in a black base coat, while long marks of purple and crimson signaled fresher applications.

Some of the prisoners in the compound were being murdered and dismembered for meat right out in the open. Right there in the dirt. Others lay dead in various states of decomposition. There were several instances of children sitting alone and crying.

A handful of Motherless gawked at the woman as the pickup parked beside a row of old classrooms. After a terse discussion, a fight broke out amongst them, a portly man wearing leather overalls declaring himself the victor.

The pickup truck driver enlisted two of the brawl's losers to usher the woman into the building and lock her in one of the classrooms, a cube reeking of sweat and urine, where six other pink-tagged women were chained to the walls. Their converters had been stapled to their faces to prevent them from committing invader-assisted suicide.

The woman cast a labored gaze over the female prisoners as the Motherless shackled her to the wall. Only two of the other women looked up at her. The other four were lifeless, one of them dead with eyelids hanging open. A stack of decade old textbooks in the corner, elementary math, peered at the women through some twisted spectacle of time.

One of the Motherless pinned the woman from behind, palming her entire head with one hand, while another approached with an industrial staple gun. The second Motherless aligned the stapler to the converter strap on the woman's cheek. She let out a pained grunt as the first staple pierced her left cheek, and again when another staple punctured the right.

The woman sat against the wall and hung her head.

Refractions of evening light streamed through a barred window, and as the commotion of the Motherless outside dissipated, muffled laments of enslaved women and children throughout the building rose like a mist of sorrow.

"Olifia? Is that you?" said the woman, sometime after night had fallen.

Olifia, one of the lifeless four, lifted a blackened eyelid from the room's corner, briefly revealing a beaming white sclera before closing it. The darkness surrounding her seemed more than an absence of light, appearing to the woman like a cave or abyss, as if Olifia existed in a space between life and death. Between reality and despair.

No one spoke or moved besides the woman, who rose to test the give of a screw by her shackle mount. The screw itself didn't budge, but its wood casing gave slightly, and the woman began chipping around the head with a dull fingernail.

Disks howled that night in a way the woman had not heard before. Three of them, all close, traded low wails that languished in the dark and brooding sky, and the Crone and her manic acolytes screeched back at them like odd wolves. The enslaved women were quiet at night when the guards weren't raping them, but the children's cries carried on. One of them even called out for his mother.

But the screw, that object of utter insignificance, was the woman's sole focus that night and for the next two days. Two days of hell for each of the prisoners in that room, even for the dead one who was only collected after the woman informed the guards of her condition. In their lust to repeatedly rape her, they had not seemed to notice.

The third night brought taps of rain down on the sagging roof. As creeping veins of water eroded the classroom's drywall, another form of erosion — the woman's bleeding fingernails — had finally picked away enough wood around the screw's head to loosen it. She took great care to twist the screw out of its socket, as if dropping it might detonate the entire world.

Rain fell harder the next day, a day the woman spent working the screw at various angles in the shackle's keyhole. It clicked open by nightfall, and she was free. She scampered through puddles over to Olifia.

"Hey," she whispered. "Let's go."

Olifia didn't move. She didn't even open her eyes. The corner she laid in was cold and damp and somehow darker than it was before, her dirty clothing and broken body seeping deeper into its blackness. "No," she said, a weak word carried more by her torrid breath than her fractured voice.

"Don't be ridiculous. Your children need you."

"They're dead."

"You don't know that."

"Then take them." Her whisper was barely audible. The staple through Olifia's left cheek had infected the skin such that bloated and pus-filled wounds crept over the edge of her converter strap.

"What? What are you talking about? Come with me. If you die like this, you're letting them win."

"I have nothing left."

"Get up, goddammit! Do you know what I wouldn't give for one more second with my kids?"

Olifia winced as she took a long, slow swallow, scant saliva clicking in her arid mouth. "Go."

"You're just gonna leave them?"

"I've been ready to die for a long time."

"Come on. I can get you—"

The slam of the outer hallway door sliced through the beats of rain, and the woman scampered back to her shackle just as the overalled man entered the room. As if fate compelled him, as if his new natural law divined him, he decided to start with the woman.

But not seconds after the man put his knees on the ground between her open legs, the woman snapped her head up to lock eyes with him. There was no fear in those eyes — only rage — as she heaved the shackle away.

She threw one leg over his neck, pinned his hand to the floor, jerked her hips up, shifted to the side, and wrenched his neck between her knees. She squeezed down on his arm and his neck with all her strength, every single ounce of power she could muster. The man's face turned as red as the rising sun, and the veins in his neck and his forehead popped through his skin like pipes about to burst. He coughed, punched her in the ribs, bucked his legs in futility. He struggled to his feet with the woman dangling from his neck and slammed her down with a thud loud enough to shake the room. But the woman's legs were too strong. A fraction of an inch at a time, she tightened, and tightened, and tightened. Little movements, large consequences. After a few minutes of choking, he lost his ability to move, spewing out a litany of spit-coated curses, then he lost consciousness. She shoved off his reeking torso away from her and climbed to her knees to catch her breath.

A crack of thunder pierced the night. A disk howled, high and shrill.

One of the other prisoners sat up. "Hey, get me out of here. Please."

Still gasping, the woman rose and tossed her the screw. "Pull it back to the right and jostle it. You'll know you have it when it clicks."

The rain intensified, streams of it trickling through the ceiling.

After checking the hall for more Motherless, she dragged her unconscious abuser out into the downpour and lugged him into the cage in the white pickup truck, the same one that had brought her here. She put on his boots and overalls, letting the clothes and rain swim over her. Using his knife, she sliced open his hand and smeared blood on her face to mimic the bedlamites in the schoolyard. She searched his pockets — now hers — finding the keys, but as she inserted the key into the ignition, something made her pause. She looked back at the hall of torture, now a blurry gray smudge in the driving rain.

"Goddammit," she said, and she clenched her molars as she opened the chamber door and trudged back inside.

In the classroom next to the one she'd escaped from, nearly a dozen children were chained to the walls. All of them were laying down or slumped in the corners, lifeless like giant dolls, green tags in their ears, staples in their little cheeks. There was something swampy, more organic about the stench in here, a moist hand that gripped the woman's throat. Odors of biological neglect had alchemically fused with those of a darker order, the invisible residue of unspeakable acts — acts of the highest evil — which hung in the air and clung to the peeling paint.

She scanned the decrepit room for a boy with sandy blond hair. He was there, in the far corner by himself, dead, clothing caked with stains of long-dried blood that looked like tar. His pants were soiled and with hardened waste.

Her boots clacked loudly as she walked across the tile, snap-snaps splashing across the room as if stepping through puddles of shame for even entering such a place.

With a hand wrapped over her convertor, she crouched over the boy's body. His eyes were open. One green, one blue. He wore a necklace, a bright collection of beads on a string. Something a child would be proud of. One of the beads was wrapped with a faded Mickey Mouse sticker. Cradling his head, she slipped the necklace off him and stuffed it into her pocket. She sighed.

On her way out, an unassuming pair of eyes arrested her. One of Olifia's two young daughters, the brunette, gazed at her in fascination. A wicked purple bruise covered more than half of her forehead.

"Oh my God," the woman said, rushing to her. She gripped the girl's knobby elbows. "Hold on. You stay right here. I'm gonna get you out. Is your sister here?"

The girl shook her head.

"Okay. I'll be right back. You stay here and you don't move."

The woman strode out to the truck, rain soaking her, and she pulled down the passenger seat to access the jack. Her abuser groaned from inside the locked cage.

Back in the classroom, the woman beat the girl's chain with the jack. Clanging metals, like twangs from a blacksmith's anvil, compelled some of the other children to life.

"Can you get me out, too?" said a soft voice. A boy, the same one who'd cried for his mother during the night.

His voice paralyzed the woman for a moment, but she shoved aside the instincts burning inside her and went on hacking the chain.

"Are we being freed?" another one said. A preteen girl.

The chain was bending but not breaking, and the woman grunted with every hammer fall of the jack. Blood on her face and arms — now less viscous from the rain — rolled into her eyes and dripped onto her working hands.

Another girl cried out in jubilation. "Hey, everyone! We're getting out of here! We're going home!"

The blood on the woman's hands weakened her grip, and after one particularly desperate blow, the jack sputtered out of her hand and twirled against the wall.

An air-raid siren blared outside. Motherless started shouting, engines started revving. The Crone, her voice already robotic enough, issued droning commands through a series of loudspeakers set up across the compound.

A couple of the children began to cry. Others celebrated. Olifia's daughter looked at them blankly, all of them looking at her.

"Quiet!" said the woman. "You guys have to stay quiet!"

The rain had intensified into a torrent of weight and water and sound. The children's energy rose with it, assessing themselves and their would-be rescuer as waterfalls gushed through holes where only small leaks had been before.

Someone outside fired a rocket launcher, and a few seconds later, the unmistakable screech of invaders quelled all sound around it. More rockets, heavy gunfire. Lots of shouting.

A couple of the children screamed, more started crying. The woman let out a yell of her own with the blow that broke the chain. She scooped up the girl and started to leave but turned around to face the children as she stood in the threshold of the door. All those desperate sets of eyes, most of them in tears, stared back at her, pleading.

A mortar blast rocked another part of the building, and now streams of dust fell from the ceiling along with the rainfall. She looked at the children in horror and tightened her arms around the girl, as if that little body was the only thing keeping her organs from spilling right out of her chest.

"I... I can't," the woman said, her voice weak. "I'm sorry."

The children raised all manner of hell through tiny converters as the woman took slow steps backwards. The brittle room filled with water, with dust, with fear. She choked out broken apologies, only loud enough for the girl in her arms to hear over the storm.

The woman closed the door behind her.

Outside, angry sheets of rain billowed through the schoolyard, their sweeps and swirls pounding the earth into a slurry, their effervescent edges cloaking the impending combatants in thin white veils of some bastardization version of holiness.

"Put your seatbelt on for me," said the woman as she dumped the girl into the truck's passenger seat, tassels of rainwater spinning down from her chin and her outstretched elbows. "I'm gonna get us out of here. Okay?"

An apocalyptic symphony engulfed the schoolyard. Wet earth trembled under the tires of mechanized beasts, acrid smoke coughed forth from corroded mufflers, and flashes of ordnance painted grotesque shadows across the landscape.

And the shrieks of invaders, those piercing and otherworldly wails, rolled forward from the back of the alien ranks to the front. That sound smothered the hearts of weaker men and tested the constitutions of the strongest.

Indeed, to engage the invaders required the severing of some cord of sanity, a reversion to one's most feral state. Down to the man, the Motherless were up to the task. Even through the blinding rain, their mobilization came swift and lethal, and whatever they lacked in organization was accounted for by their fanaticism for death.

Most of the Motherless on foot wielded both a firearm and a piercing weapon, employing a seemingly well-rehearsed maneuver of striking an invader from distance with gunfire, charging, and then driving blades or sharpened poles down its open throat. The soldiers moved in groups of four or five to engage one invader at a time, most skirmishes resulting in at least one human casualty. Sometimes a soldier would sacrifice themselves so the rest of the group could attack. Sometimes an invader would just kill them all. Their plated bodies deflected an untold number of bullets, and a single well-placed swipe of their claws could tear through three humans in close proximity.

Back in the schoolyard, a hydroplaning van toppled over the tallest mountain of cages. They clattered to the ground and stuck motionless in the mud. Prisoners that survived the impact screamed and flailed through in their wire coffins, while a river of blood gaining steam and volume flowed under their bodies. The river gushed down towards the main gate, where it mixed with several other bloody tributaries tentacled throughout the compound.

Rockets and gun turrets pounded the alien vanguard as they assaulted the gates, and fighting vehicles flanked groups of invaders coagulated along the outer walls, pummeling them with heavy fire from behind. The invaders were hoarding up from the valley, hundreds of them churning as a single mass, a terrible red wave rising in a sea of rain. The walls of the compound buckled under their sheer volume. Each invader would charge kamikaze into the backs of the ones in front of it, smacking chrome against chrome, using their collective strength to bend the walls a little further.

Then, the walls broke, and the red wave poured in. It washed over every man, woman, child, and object in the schoolyard.

The woman's pickup truck was mere feet from the gate when two invaders leapt onto the cab. She careened it around three Motherless, one of them armless, stabbing an invader with spears.

The girl screamed.

"Hold on!"

The woman wrenched the steering wheel to the side as she rounded the edge of the broken gate, spinning one of the invaders to the ground. When the other climbed over onto the hood and peered through the windshield, the girl screamed again, and the woman slammed on the brakes to send it hurtling forward. She stomped both feet onto the gas pedal and smacked the invader with the left side of the fender.

As they sputtered out the gate towards freedom, the Crone's final order over loudspeakers headed away from the action. Two vehicles followed it towards a small gap in the back of the camp, and they spilled out, undetected.

One by one, each of the compound's buildings exploded, decimating structure, Motherless, prisoner, and invader alike into a hazy white maw that consumed all the sky and the country.

She drove east for the better part of the day, peeling off the highway when an abandoned barn drew within sight. It stood out against the naked landscape like a wooden ghost, two rectangular windows below the roofline for eyes and a black gaping mouth where a door once was. The sky was so gray, so vacant, it seemed to not be there at all, and the only vestiges of life out in the expanse were the wispy calls of evening insects, vague sounds that seemed more ethereal than acoustic.

After nightfall, she prepared a bed for the girl from the cushions of the pickup's seat. She unfastened the tag in the girl's ear, and the girl unfastened the woman's. She knelt over the girl, wiping the hair away from her eyes. "I'll find something to get those staples out in the morning."

The girl's face was red and dirty, her eyes puffy from latent tears.

"Hey," said the woman. "It's gonna be okay. We're gonna eat good tomorrow. You like mushrooms?"

"Is my mom gone?"

The woman sighed.

The girl began to cry.

She laid down next to the girl, held her. "Oh, sweetheart. I know. I know. I do know that pain."

The girl clutched her back.

The woman looked at the girl. "You know what? I'm just like you, okay? Everyone in my family is gone. Everyone. It's unfortunately not that rare. You're not alone."

The girl only cried harder.

"I know some good people who will take care of you. You'll—"

"Can I stay with you?"

The question froze the woman.

"Aren't you just like me? You're all alone, right?"

The woman smiled under her converter. "Let's just get through tonight."

In that lonely hour, the girl fell asleep in the woman's arms and the night receded into itself. The insects drew down their calls. A full moon crept out from behind its veil of cloud cover. The woman laid there with eyes open. Thinking, waiting.

When the time was right, she snaked her arm from under the girl, rose, and stepped outside. The hinging squeal of the truck door was a murderous wail in that hollow and dead quiet night. The woman started the engine. She drove. Not far, but far enough.

"Step outside," she said to the abuser while opening the cage, tire iron dangling from her right hand.

His face was hidden in shadow. He whispered something to her, faint words that slithered into the fabric of her heart where they would dwell until she took her final breath.

"If you don't come out of that cage, I'm gonna drag you out and kill you."

Still, the man didn't move. A deafening silence passed, the pressure between them boiling. He laughed, and he repeated what he said before. A ship howled far off to the east.

The woman lunged for his foot, grabbed it, yanked him out of the cage. He hit the ground with a thud, and it was there that she killed him. It required three blows to the head to take the man's life but twelve to fulfill her measure of justice. The tire iron made no sound dropped it in the grass.

She spent some time seated against the truck's grill, alone, catching her breath, gazing up into the moonlight.

PART 3

HEALTHY AND STRONG

The brilliance of an autumn sunrise in the Rockies is a vision that lingers in one's memory, especially from atop a 14,000-foot peak. Blankets of light and dark sky erupt into an impossible vastness, depths that conjure the contemplation of one's terrifying smallness and the more transient elements of our nature. Loose gray rocks, bland and cryptic things as old as time, watch with you, delighting in the chance to share their secrets for a brief while. The Colorado Plateau is laid bare. Forests, deserts, rivers, more mountains, even the curve of the earth, all seen through the macroscopic lens of a deity.

Not so long ago, those that found this land in the days of its innocence used these peaks to chart their own path to divinity. All that remains of them now is the errant charm or talisman, things once touched by man now smoothed and faded and mixed in with the natural treasures that the gods may compel in a more timeless ceremony.

It starts in twilight, when a ruddy line grips the horizon and bubbles up into a glowing neon rim. A boiling orb pokes through the earth's plane and slowly rises, as if conjured, and its gradual ascent splashes the sky with elated reds and purples that stretch on through infinity. Cirrus clouds find their crinkle from capillaries of light bleeding around their edges. You may hear the cut of the wind, or if you're lucky, the caws of raptors who were there before you and will be there long after you leave.

"You can see five states from here," said the woman. She leaned in closer to the girl and gestured far out over the waking earth. Their sleeping bags were nestled close to each other, sharing their warmth, their safety. "Colorado, New Mexico, Nebraska, Kansas, Wyoming. Way over there is Oklahoma."

The girl wiped her converter-less mouth, staple-scars in her cheeks now fully healed. "What's states?"

"It was a way people used to divide up the land."

"Which one is your favorite?"

"Well, I'm not from any of them. I don't really have a favorite but I think about them often."

The girl rubbed her eyes. "I like the last one."

"Oklahoma?"

"Yeah."

"You've never been to Oklahoma."

She shrugged, twig-like shoulders rising only inches. "I like how it sounds."

They took their time rising. The woman sat on a flat rock and cracked her neck and meditated. The girl pulled out a coloring book from her backpack and started drawing with black and red crayons, the only two she had. They drank and washed their converters with one of their three bottles of water, and they ate sticks of magpie jerky in the early morning light.

"It'll be winter soon," said the woman. "We need to get you some proper clothes. Were you warm enough last night?"

The girl nodded, not looking up from her work.

"That means I'm gonna have to leave you for a couple of days."

She stopped coloring. "What?"

"I have to go to some place where it's not safe to get supplies."

The girl looked up with a face of exasperation. "Can I please come? You never take me."

"It's way too dangerous."

"But I need to learn how to handle dangerous places."

"The best way to handle dangerous places is to avoid them."

"What's unsafe about it?"

"We've been over this."

"I can handle myself around invaders. I know how to stay quiet and hide."

"I'm not taking the risk. Besides, we have a lot to do to prepare the cabin before the first frost, and I could really use your help while I'm gone."

"What if the Crone gets me again?"

"Don't be believing what that man said at 115. Even if she is still alive she doesn't have her army."

The girl scoffed, a habit she'd picked up from her caretaker. "She doesn't need an army. I'm just one girl."

They hiked out in the late morning, saying little to each other, as both watched their footfalls over the steep downhill grade. The woman instructed the girl to put her converter back on when they reached the tree line. Their path took them through a sap-scented forest of colossal pines, feet crunching lightly on blankets of pine needles.

Before continuing after a bathroom break, the woman put a halting hand out to the girl and then cupped her ear and pointed up. Two woodpeckers buzzed in the trees, one of them directly above her. In absolute silence, the woman pulled a slingshot from her bag and handed it to the girl. She crouched beside her.

"Remember what I taught you," she whispered. "Where's the pitch?"

"It's really high."

"Okay. Remember to hold your breath on the release."

The slingshot was professional grade, black metal frame with a vinyl wrist harness. The girl placed a round ball in its holster, lined it up, and fired. The ammo sailed off into the sky, missing the woodpecker and the tree it tapped on. The woodpecker paused for a moment, sensing something awry.

"That's okay. You know what you did wrong?"

The girl nodded. She was already lining up another shot. This one hit the woodpecker and sent it faltering to the ground.

"Well done!" said the woman. "You're getting good." She gathered the woodpecker, bleeding and squirming, feathers gone from its whole bottom half. "Want me to do the hard part?"

The girl shook her head.

Like a priestess distributing her Eucharist, she handed over the bird. The girl stared at it for a moment and exhaled, her head bent reverently. "Thank you, God, for providing this gift. My mom and I will use it well. We will use it to keep ourselves…" She looked up at the woman.

"Healthy and strong."

"Healthy and strong. Amen." The girl closed her eyes and twisted the bird's neck through a series of tight little cracks.

The woman took it from her and wrapped it in a plastic bag. "I'm very proud of you."

"See? I can handle difficult stuff."

"You're not coming with me to the mall. That's final, understand?" She tousled the girl's hair. "Come on. There's hot cocoa waiting for us at home."

The grade lost much of its severity as the pines morphed into golden aspens. Beams from the noonday sun soaked through every yellow leaf around them, dipping the world into a crisp and ambered glow, lighting the way to the base. They threw down their packs upon reaching a crystal-clear stream, a shimmering ribbon of light and sound slicing through brown beds of earth. A beady lizard ran over one of the rocks. The woman refilled their water bottles and dropped in iodine tablets. The girl washed her face and stared at the water.

"You remember what these trees are called?"

The girl looked up. "Aspens."

"And what's special about aspens?"

"Are those the ones that are really old?"

"You're thinking of redwoods. Try again."

"How old are the redwoods?"

"Thousands of years. We're not even really sure."

"How many times have they survived the invaders?"

"These invaders are the first to ever come here."

"Do you think they'll be the last?"

The woman regained her pack and took two large swigs from one of the water bottles. She tossed another bottle to the girl. "Aspens," she said. "What's special about these trees?"

The girl didn't answer until they reached the trailhead and were galloping across the parking lot. "Oh! They're the ones with the crazy roots."

"That's right. They look like many trees, but they're actually one giant organism. They feed off the same soil. They help each other."

They tossed their packs in the back of the white pickup stolen from the Crone's compound, the bed now cageless. The woman kicked one of the tires and popped the hood after turning over the engine. "Shit."

"What's wrong?" said the girl.

"You stay here in the truck and lock it up. I'll be right back."

The woman closed the hood and strode over to a pair of park service vans that hadn't moved in over a decade. Mold crept over the windows and rust ate away at the panels. Mossy undergrowth thrived under all eight deflated tires.

She reached through the broken windshield of the first van and engaged the hood trigger. Weeds hid and strangled most of the machinery inside. She looked back at the girl, then back down. After clearing away most of the growth over the engine, she slipped off the belt and held it up to the light. It was rock hard, crumbling to nothing in her fingers after she tested its give. She scoffed and went back to the truck.

They took off their converters and drove.

Prismatic vistas out of the driver's side window tempted the woman's gaze away from the winding switchback road. There were sprawling forests of pine, crystal blue lakes, pale rock formations basking in the afternoon sun. There were no disks.

The girl kept her nose in her coloring book, working the red and black crayons down to nubs. Even as the jagged road attempted to misguide her hand, her sketching never strayed outside the lines.

Dusk had settled by the time they veered off the high road and onto a craggy reach of unmarked land. They drove up a long hill, through a palisade of pines, and parked next to a timber frame cabin that overlooked a river and more mountains, mountains whose faces had turned evening black.

The girl put her converter back on, threw open her door, and ran into the cabin. Vegetables grew in planter boxes of well-tilled soil by the door — squash, onions, zucchini, cucumber, carrots, kale — all cordoned off from the wilderness by a split-rail fence lined in chicken wire. Between the cabin and the river lay a field of wheatgrass and wildflowers, the oncoming night not yet powerful enough to squelch its multi-colored celebration.

"Hey! Am I unpacking alone?" shouted the woman. She sighed and hauled both of their bags inside.

The girl, now equipped with a yellow crayon, was hunched over her coloring book at a table in the back of the main room.

"Wanna at least start a fire?" said the woman.

The girl paid her no mind.

"Excuse me? Did you go deaf?"

"Sorry," said the girl. She slid off her chair and grabbed two logs and a starter from a pile next to an old stove.

The woman struck a match and lit candles. Dozens of them sat on tables, on shelves, in cups strewn throughout the place. Last, she lit the fire the girl had prepared.

It wasn't a large cabin — a living room with a hearth and kitchen, a separate bedroom, a bathroom that didn't function, a closet. Timbers old and dusty, floors that groaned under their footsteps. The windows were small and thin, letting in more cold than light, and the door only stayed closed with something lodged against it. The woman had attempted and given up constructing an air filtration system like the one she'd seen at Elijah's, and now the project gathered dust on a desk by the fireplace.

As they did most nights, they ate roasted vegetables and drank purified river water. After the main meal, the woman cooked the woodpecker. She took a bottle of honey from a shelf bursting with mason jars, most containing pickled vegetables, and slathered the strips of meat with a thick coat. They ate the strips together in silence, carefully pulling down their converters to take bites.

Before bed, they climbed a ladder to the roof, where the woman gave the girl a guided tour of the stars. She held the girl's head in the crook of her arm.

"If you get separated from me, you can use the stars to find your way home. All that we know and see is known and seen by those stars. They're so old you can't even imagine it. They're watching us, guiding us. Don't let your heart sink if you can't see them one night, or two nights, or even ten. They'll always come back and they'll never let you down. I love them for that."

They laid there for a long time as the river babbled and the night cooled. Loud sighs sputtered from the girl's converter. The woman held her tighter.

Out on the river, an owl on long range patrol screeched and took off across the field. It sailed like a white, floating wisp through the moonglow on the water, flapping its heavy wings and bobbing through the air in near perfect time with the rhythm of the woman's heart. She tracked it with her eyes as it rose and fell over the treetops, then she looked back up to the stars.

They were one with the land out here, the woman and the girl. They touched it, tilled it, breathed it, smelled it. It fed them and it healed them, and it lived in them as much as they lived in it. Its dirt settled in their pores and under their fingernails, its sunlight blazoned their skin. The grass and the trees and the river gifted them limitless coffers of food and supply, and the soil did as they commanded. The birds sang, and the fields danced, and the river rolled softly to a tune set forth by the rocks in its bed, a porcelain music box of pattern and liquid.

And even though the woman had memorized the constellations, she never missed a chance to be with them. She sought them out and looked upon their faces, for they shone brighter in her heart than they did in her eyes, and only to bear them witness was to actually see them. Many a night did she sneak across the cabin floor and tiptoe to the roof alone.

"There are many wonders amongst the stars," she whispered.

That night, the disks did not howl, but the girl did. It had become a common occurrence, the girl calling out to her family, teleporting through nightmares back to those screams, that compound, that campsite from hell. The woman rolled over in the bed and embraced the girl. She held her, hushed her, loved her.

"Please don't leave me," the girl said.

"I would never, my dear. I would never."

The girl's sobs faded to heaving coos on the edge of the night until finally she fell silent. The woman stayed there, and in the dream, her oldest child came to her.

Low fade haircut like his father's. Front teeth only half-grown in. Chestnut eyes that when the light hit them burned like flames. A serious face. A gentle heart.

He sat at the kitchen table in one of the four matching chairs her husband had bought on sale.

"You know those chairs weren't really on sale?" she had said, smirking. "The price of two is really just the price of four. They always cost that much."

He scoffed.

Her son was drawing a picture with a yellow crayon, motions steady and deliberate. His younger sister entered the room, flitting across the floor like a small bell. She sat at the table and started pelting him with kernels of cereal. In the other room, the baby started crying. The woman couldn't see her husband, but she could hear his voice as he recounted a story from when they were young. Her daughter got up and tried to give the baby cereal.

The woman only had eyes for her son. Although she stood by his side, he was far away from her. So very far. He stopped, cutting off his coloring motion mid-stroke. He looked at her. Another world lived in those eyes now, smoky pearls where nebulas shrank to the size of marbles, worlds of memories blurred and wilted.

"There you are," she said. "I've been looking all over for you."

He held up the picture—

When sparrow songs tickled the woman's ears at dawn, her heart was filled with love, a wise and distant love wrung from the threads that still bound her to her children, a love that bled into the warmth of the girl in her arms.

They woke together, blinking away sunbeams dancing on the river. The girl clicked saliva around in her converter-clad mouth and sat up in bed, silhouetting herself in the old weather-beaten window. Sharp autumn gusts whistled through gaps in the timbers, and the honks of migrating geese bounced off the slopes they coasted over. The woman looked up at their chevron formation as it disappeared into the sky, and then looked at the girl and put a hand on her back.

"Is my head bleeding?" said the girl.

"No. Why would you think that?"

"I dreamt that it was."

The woman swung her bare feet out of bed and spilled them onto the frigid floorboards. "We've gotta get ready to go. I'm gonna take us to go see someone first. He might have what we need."

"Who?"

"A friend. He's safe."

Nose already just inches away from the window, the girl leaned in further. Her gaze drew sharper, more intense, as if the rising sun itself — or something else out there — called to her.

"Can you get the jugs for me this morning?" said the woman.

The girl didn't answer. Although the morning's light shone brightly around her, she sat pensive and shrouded in a kind of darkness.

The woman leaned over and planted her arms on either side of the girl. "You want to sleep a little more while I set up the irrigation? You can check the traps later."

She nodded.

The woman took a long look at the girl. "You doin' alright?"

She nodded again, an identical little wag of the chin, a child's motion.

"Wanna talk about what hap—"

"No."

The woman leaned back and glared at the wall where the wind seeped in, then looked at the girl again. "It's okay to talk about bad things. Sometimes it helps you feel better."

The girl was still there, and the sun, rising headlong in the waking sky, illuminated the bed they sat on.

"You want your coloring books?"

The girl said nothing, made no gesture to acknowledge the question.

The woman reached for the girl's hand but stopped herself. Heat no longer emanated from that tiny body, only cold.

She went into the living room and lit a fire and ate some of the vegetables from last night. The fireplace was still warm, and it didn't take much persuasion to get the coals to spark and light two fresh logs. She splashed water over her face and shaved her head, and then she sat down on the ground and did pushups, sit-ups, and stretched out her legs. She meditated to the crackling fire and the tinny chitters of swallows hashing out parochial concerns above the chimney.

The outside — fresh and woody — greeted the woman when she opened the door. Her eyes tracked over that sprawling wilderness: dewy grass, ruddy trees, a blurry horizon where autumn mists cooled the sky into a celadon haze.

She strode to a small shed some ways off, opened the old door, and gathered a dozen empty milk jugs into a wheelbarrow. After wheeling them back to the cabin, she filled them all with water from a large tank attached to the outside wall and nestled one jug into each planter box in the vegetable garden. Tiny drops seeped out of microscopic holes in the plastic and into the soil. She made two more round trips from the shed to the garden, gathering enough jugs to assign one to each plant in her care.

The woman called to the girl to meet her by the river, and the girl burst out the door and bounded through the upstream field with arms outstretched. Each stalk of wheatgrass that grazed the child held in awkward place for a moment, standing as if her touch was a means to catalog them. Wildflowers dotted the field by the riverbank, flowers the girl and the woman had spent many afternoons picking. Sitting in the silence of the summer's warmth, they'd stitch flower rings and chains and ropes that now decorated their hearth and home.

The girl squatted by the bank and reached into the lapping water, and hand over fist began yanking a rope lashed to a pole in the mud. The woman arrived at her side by the time the wire of the trap drew within sight under the water's surface.

"Empty!" said the girl, releasing the rope and darting further up the bank.

Strain broke out over the girl's face as she jerked on the next rope, to no avail. The woman gripped a section of line fist deep in the water. She used her whole body to heave the rope back. The girl grunted behind her, pulling but not necessarily helping, and she gasped when the trap and its contents appeared.

"Ha! Look at that!" said the woman. She unlatched the cage and held out a yellow perch as big as her forearm. The fish thrashed in the woman's grip, but her hands were strong.

Together, they checked five more traps and secured two more fish. The woman brought their catch into the kitchen, and lording over a cutting board and a whetstone, cured them and packed the cutlets into a salt-layered crate. She closed the crate, heaved it into the bed of the pickup, and before fetching the girl, eyed warily the disk floating in the eastern sky. The girl sat on the roof of the cabin, frozen in fascination by two squirrels in the boughs of a pine tree.

"Hey," said the woman, pointing up at the disk. "That wasn't there yesterday, was it?"

"Those squirrels lost their babies."

The woman turned around. "What?"

"The mama is sad."

The woman sighed. "I know. We gotta go, though. We're gonna be on the road at night if we don't leave and I don't remember seeing that disk yesterday. Can you please come down?"

The girl obeyed.

They drove out of the valley and into the conjoining lands, where fall foliage glimmered against the backdrop of the prairie, where yellow blanket flowers waltzed on low-lying scrubland to the call of a gathering wind. Out to the south, the road flanked a vast reservoir, a barren place free from any tree, bush, or sign of natural life. All that stood as evidence of its presence was a barbed wire fence so rusty it seemed to consume the noonday light. The rocks around the banks were black and volcanic, angry looking things cursing all who might dare behold them. To the east of the reservoir, a weary old house sat choking in kudzu and wilting from neglect, and floating high above, a lone hawk had calibrated the headwind so precisely it appeared suspended in space, flapping its great wings only once while they drove past.

"Can I ask a favor?" said the woman.

"What?"

"We're gonna pass the place where I met you. Do you remember that place?"

The girl nodded with some degree of disdain, her eyes still on the hawk.

"I was wondering if I could go back and get something I left there. Something that means a lot to me."

"What is it?"

"It's a pouch of little things that remind me of some people that I loved. I feel better when it's close to me, sort of like you with your coloring books. You know what I mean?"

"I really don't wanna go back there."

"Well, I don't either, but—"

"You said it yourself to stay out of dangerous places."

The woman slammed on the brakes. "Shit!"

"What's wrong?"

She pointed out the windshield at a group of four invaders motoring across the prairie. They were just dots out there, but their limbs spun in such a fury that they blurred together in a deathly red vapor steaming on the edge of the meridian.

In the speed of almost a single motion, the woman turned off the engine — right in the middle of the road — crammed the girl's body under the glove box and laid tight over her trembling back.

“Stay down,” she whispered. “Just stay down and stay calm. Be quiet.”

The echoes of their battle cries caromed off the mountains and assaulted the pickup from every direction, descending from the peaks like the calls of apocalyptic horsemen, and they blended with the hyperbolic death march of hooves drumming in soil.

The girl began to cry. The woman hushed her.

The alien shrieks grew louder, angrier, so close now that whatever heinous vocal mechanism produced them revealed their true nature: thousands of sharp trills that in the space of a second melted into a single, chaotic scream.

The invaders passed right by, almost through, and the pickup jostled in the wake of their brushback. The girl let out a yelp as the woman held her tighter, shrieks charging onward to some unknowable destination.

“They didn’t see us,” she said. “They almost hit us, but they didn’t see us.”

The entrance to Comm 445 hadn’t changed much since the woman’s last visit. Autumn had turned its kelly green shroud to bronze. Yellow leaves littered its road, beckoning travelers towards a golden destination. Guards stood at their same stations — on the road, in the trees, at the gate — and they gave the woman and the girl no trouble upon entry.

Few clues of the spring attack that left so many dead remained. No blood on the roads. Guards plentiful and buoyant. Even the walls, once smashed and splintered from those alien battering rams, had either been replaced with new timbers or buttressed with more metal plates and barbed wire. Children were more numerous than they were just a few short months ago. They ran in small packs through the dirty gravel streets and harried the elders for whatever treats might rattle in their pockets. The girl watched the children with her nose pressed against the glass of the truck window like a zoo animal, like an alien herself in observation of their foreign cadences.

"You stay with me when we're walking around here, okay?" said the woman.

Regis was hunched over a hookah in a blue canopy tent next to his shipping container. He eyed the white truck with some level of hostility until the woman got out.

"The hell'd you get that old beater?" Regis said, rising.

"You don't wanna know."

"Where have you been? I got that faring you wanted. You still want it?"

The woman opened the passenger door, and the girl got out, and Regis crouched to bring his eyes level with the child. He smiled, age lines creasing his cheeks under a pale-yellow converter. His movements were spry, but his face was old and grizzled, brow stony and strong from all it had weathered, eagle eyes that, when squinted, seemed to sense colors buried far beneath the girl's complexion. He wore the same exact pea coat and jeans.

"And who might you be?" he said softly.

Later that evening, the guards shuffled groups of civilians out of the streets and into the plaza. Their captain held a finger tight to the trigger of a bullhorn and barked orders as if an invasion might materialize straight out of the oncoming night. Civilians retreated to whence they came, leaving the roads open only for official traffic and communication. A yellow siren light mounted on a truck cab blipped down the darkening road, and stenches of the dead rose from the truck's bed. Several of the guards turned and regarded it. One took off his hat and bowed his head.

All roads in 445 wound like entrails through the comm and converged at the central plaza. When the guards had cleared the streets, civilians poured in and shared food, music, conversation, and firelight. No sudden movements, no rising voices. All these bodies flickered yellow and orange around their fires, as if embers themselves pulsing in the night, lifeforms vibrant yet fleeting and reduced.

"So now that you've got company, you holing up somewhere permanent?" said Regis. He sat beside the woman on the circular steps rimming the plaza, overlooking the heart of the commune as it beat before them. The girl was asleep in a cat-like ball at their feet.

"There's an old cabin on the bank of the river a bit west of here," she said.

"Off that grassy turnoff on the mountain highway?"

She looked at him, puzzled.

"I know there's good fishing up that way, and you brought me a hell of a lot of fish."

"Creep."

He laughed.

"Do me a favor and don't tell anyone, okay?"

"I won't if you keep bringing me those fish."

The woman began rolling a cigarette.

"You know, I could get you those parkas if you waited here a few weeks," he said.

"I'd rather just get it over with."

"It's dangerous as all get out up there. And that's coming from me."

The woman took a drag. She closed her eyes on the exhale, piping a smooth column of smoke from her converter's filter.

"There's really nothing I can say to make you stay, is there?"

She shook her head.

Regis swept away the side of his robe and jammed his hand into his pocket, pulling out a silver-rimmed coin with a gold center and a "2" engraved on its face. He placed it on the woman's knee.

She looked at him.

"An old Euro. Remember those? Flip it over," he said, pointing to the coin.

The letters FREIHEIT had been scratched into the hard nickel. "What is this?"

"That coin found its way here from Germany. I just got it today."

"Bullshit."

"There's a bunch of them floating around."

"Bullshit."

"Not bullshit." He plucked the cigarette from the woman's offering hand and took two quick drags. "Most of Europe is under control. The Chinese have apparently liberated Beijing, and parts of Siberia have been abandoned completely."

"How could you possibly know that?"

"Haven't you noticed? Fewer disks, fewer attacks."

The woman did not return Regis' gaze, instead tracking a man in a weathered pink sweater shuffling from fire to fire. The man was beset, wandering alone as if completely lost. He said something to a group around a fire, and while all initially regarded him, one by one they turned away as he spoke. The last to regard him — a young woman — handed him the remainder of her meal and shooed him away.

"A scouting party that nearly pulverized my pickup truck on the way over here. They're not gone, Regis. Someone's giving you the runaround."

"We haven't been attacked in months. Sightings on the western flank are falling off a cliff, and we hear they're sticking to enclosed spaces. Sure, they're not gone completely, but they're leaving." He shifted his weight towards her. "Can't you feel it?"

The girl stirred at their feet, a chill whipping through the plaza. Regis took off his pea coat and laid it over her. The dog tags around his neck jangled as he sat back down. "We can keep her warm here. We can keep you safe here. A few weeks is all I'm asking. Maybe you can't feel it yet, but I can. The winds are shifting. The invaders are leaving.

Give it a month or two at the most, and I bet we'll be able to browse those warehouses like nothing ever happened."

"Like nothing ever happened."

"There's no reason for you to go down there. Really, there's not."

"I'll be fine. I know how to handle them better than anyone."

He sighed. "If Jason were here right now, he'd—"

As if spring-loaded, the woman recoiled and jammed a forefinger into Regis' face. "Don't. Don't you dare."

A pair of minstrels bearing a guitar and a handheld harp ascended the outer plaza stairs, weaving through civilians. They didn't interrupt their song while offering Regis and the woman long, loping bows before moving on. The woman kept staring at the ragged man. She pointed to him.

"Do you see that man down there? Last time I was here, he begged me to help him find his son. Said he had nothing left, that all that mattered to him anymore was finding his boy. I found him at the Crone's, dead in a corner in the same room I found her, abused and emaciated and lying in a pool of his own blood. There must have been a dozen kids in that room. They had tags in their ears, like cattle. A hell if I've ever seen one." She retrieved Mickey's necklace from her pocket and placed it on Regis' knee. "What do you think happens to this world if they leave?"

"We rebuild."

She shook her head. "I was there, Regis. I'm almost positive she escaped. She's out there somewhere, rebuilding her army. And if she's not, only a matter of time before someone else does."

Three masked people darted out of a side street and into the plaza. They barely stopped moving as they robbed a group of families their food and belongings, and they were gone by the time the guards even began chasing.

Regis rose, gave her back the necklace. He pointed to the coin. "It means 'Freedom.'" He turned away, shuffled through the plaza, and evaporated into the crowd. Just another body, another ember burning in the night.

The minstrels were gone. Many of the fires were out, their makers returned to their homes and their shacks. The night was cold. The sky was starless. Even the nocturnal flyers — bats and owls and swifts and nightjars — were silent, as if collectively heeding some conspiratorial decree.

She would see Regis again that night in a black and blue nightmare, where cloud and smoke overlaid a backdrop of sprawling urban carnage. A thick swarm of invaders festered on the roof and the walls of an aircraft hangar behind her. The base of the hangar was on fire. She and the other remnants of the wing's command now escaped in armored vehicles, columns of them streaming in retreat, driving over anything in their path.

Another swarm came in from the east and laid waste to most of the other armored vehicles, myriad red monsters flowing together in a tsunami of destruction, sweeping the vehicles out to sea and drowning them in a brand of killing that could only be extraterrestrial. Three fighter jets in tight formation barreled towards the hangar and fired missiles that dropped from their bays and hung in the air for a moment before screeching forward in supersonic anger. The missiles slammed into the burning side of the hangar, charring dozens of invaders while reducing the once prideful building into a heap of smoldering metal and ash. Some invaders, maybe a hundred, climbed up the rubble and leapt up into the path of three low-flying fighter jets, turning two of them into clouds of fire on impact. The pilot of the third ejected moments before an invader clamped onto the aircraft and ripped a hole straight through the cockpit, but another invader snatched the pilot like a child with an insect and destroyed him. And as the soul inside her husband left his body, it morphed into a giant and towering apparition deep into the mountains, and it roamed there.

The woman scampered over the back seat of the vehicle she rode in. She tried to crawl through the missing rear window. Regis, seated next to her, grabbed her legs and tried to pull her back in. Regis's lieutenant — in the passenger seat — turned around and shouted something that could not be heard over the screeches of the invaders. In her mania, the woman gripped the frame where shards of glass remained and sliced open her hands. Rivers of blood poured out from streaked incisions on her palms. Blood coated her arms, and then her entire body, and then seeped into her eyes and her nose and her mouth. Everything — the sky, the burning base, her husband — turned red.

"Hey," a soft voice said.

The woman jostled awake. The morning sun blasted her eyes and the swirl of the plaza's cold, hard ground sent cruel shivers through her stiff and languid body.

"I remember you," said the man in the pink sweater, his feral-looking head blocking most of the sun. "I'm Jonah. Remember? You're that messenger."

The woman groaned as she lifted her neck to find the girl still asleep on the steps below. She looked at her hands. No blood.

He pointed at the necklace on the ground next to the woman. "That… that's his necklace! Did you find Mickey? Did you find my son?"

The woman sat up and cleared the sun from her eyes. "Yeah, I did."

Jonah held the necklace in his hands like a rosary, anxiously rubbing the beads. "Where is he? What happened?"

The girl stirred awake. The woman looked at her.

"He didn't make it, Jonah."

Jonah's hands stopped. His eyes went cold.

The woman regarded him. "Do you want to know the details?"

After a long moment, his hands found their way out of their stupor and trembled. Tears welled in his eyes. A sad howl leapt out of his heart.

With both hands, he yanked the necklace apart, beads scattering on the ground.

"I'm sor—"

He cut her off with something between a scream and a growl, and then he turned away.

The woman watched him. "I'm sorry," she whispered.

The girl picked up the bead with the Mickey Mouse sticker.

They approached the mall from the north, arching wide behind Comm 445 and weaving through side roads and dirt patches like a bird of prey zeroing in on a carcass. The only birds they saw, though, were a pair of magpies basking in their flagrant nature on a telephone wire. They had claimed the only section of wire still suspended over the chalky beige scrubland, the rest of it frayed or lying in the dirt under the collapsed poles that once held it aloft. When the pickup passed the magpies, they disbanded into the sun's paper lantern glow. Their dull calls made the silent things around them somehow even more lifeless.

"We can go if you want to," said the girl.

The woman kept her eyes on the road. "Go where?"

"To that place you wanted to go to get your special thing. You know, that place where they attacked us."

The woman took a long look out at the horizon. She put her hand on the girl's knee. She looked at the staple wound in her left cheek, now almost completely healed. "That's okay. I don't think I really need it anymore."

They passed over a rusted-out road bridge. The woman slowed the pickup to a crawl to glide over the bridge's uneven slats, making as little noise as possible.

The girl dropped the Mickey Mouse bead into a cup holder by her elbow and looked out the window. An old entrance sign adorned with a dozen rectangular labels stood as a meekish greeter to the mall's parking lot, most of the store names written on it now illegible from weather and overgrowth.

Weeds had all but conquered the mall's crumbling asphalt lot. The pickup's tires gnawed on the loose black gravel, crunching and lurching forward. The woman parked at the back of the lot, some distance away from the mall. She sat there and stared at the building.

Its sharper edges had all been dulled or broken. The roof sagged. Walls splintered with cracks where vines and other sprawling green entanglements hadn't yet taken over. Anything resembling a door or window was busted clean out, and any remnants of broken glass had been swallowed up by earth and time. A sapling grew right in the threshold of the mall's entrance.

The place was deader than the skeletons that lay inside it, yet the woman remained at a distance, hunched back in her seat as if anticipating its reaction to her presence.

"Okay," she said. "I'm gonna go in through that main door and come out the same way. If the parkas are where I remember them, it'll only be a minute or two."

"Am I staying here?"

"Yes. I don't want you anywhere near that place. You're already too close for my comfort."

She snatched the keys out of the ignition and held them in front of the girl's face.

"Remember what I told you?" she said. The woman put the keys back in the ignition and pantomimed turning them, "Turn," then she pressed the gas pedal with her foot, "Press," and gripped the steering wheel in her hands, "Steer."

The girl nodded. "I remember."

"Say it with me."

"Turn, press, steer," they said in unison.

"What side is the brake pedal? Left, or right?"

"Um, left."

"Good. Stop, left. Go, right."

The girl nodded.

"Say it with me."

Together, again: "Stop, left. Go right."

"And where will you go?"

"To the biggest road I can find."

"And what will you do when you get there?"

"Drive on the road until I find a person."

"What happens if you get lost or run out of gas?"

"Um..."

"Stay on the road, no matter what. Hide in here and lock the doors and get out when you see a car. Okay?"

"Okay."

"You got it?"

"Yeah."

"It's very important. All of it one more time for me. Ready?"

The girl took the keys from the woman's hand. "Turn, press, steer. Stop, left. Go right."

"Okay." The woman looked down and exhaled long and slow. "I'll be right back. I love you."

"I love you, too."

The woman stepped out of the pickup and closed the door with the softest of clicks, and then she went to the back to retrieve a hunting rifle and flashlight, two items she'd procured from Regis in exchange for the fish. She blew a tight dart of breath into the rifle's scope to clear any dust, opened the bolt, stacked four cartridges into the magazine, smacked the bolt shut with her palm, loaded another cartridge into the chamber, and slung the rifle over her shoulder. With her thumb under the rifle's strap by her armpit and the flashlight dangling from her other hand, she crept forward through the lot. She looked back at the girl. The girl, who was looking at her.

When she continued, her pace was even slower, even quieter, her feet deliberate, and her eyes magnetized to the mall. Her fingers grazed the sapling in the doorway, as if to verify it was no hallucination.

Inside, the mall's one great chamber was a dank and dusty time capsule. The floor was half tile, half greenery, the walls crumbling and still marked in places with the blood of those that were slain here, streaks long and grim like ghostly shadows slinking through some purgatoric gallery. Beams of noonday light poured down through fissures in the roof, and motes of dust twisted through them, tracing the light upward as if seeking their own escape from this place.

The woman pointed the flashlight at a broken escalator, and with painstaking care, placed her feet heel to toe up each step. Nearly to the second floor, something shuffled on the ground below, and she whipped around and held her breath. Nothing stared back at her save for the piles of wood, trash, and concrete chum that lay strewn about. She exhaled and checked the bars on her converter.

Slightly faster now, she strode across a second-floor sky bridge and crouched through a human-sized hole cut out of the chain link security door of an outdoors store. All the merchandise on the front shelves had been burglarized, their premium placements now occupied by dandelions and other tenants of a leafy nature. Behind the counter, there was a human skeleton curled up in a ball, still wearing the green vest its host had died in. The woman remained silent as she paced through more thin beams of light streaming through holes in the roof. All she could hear was the intensifying thump of her heartbeat. It grew heavier, faster, graver as her eyes scanned the aisles.

Most items in the outerwear section had been picked bare, but a few parkas in child's sizes remained. She set the flashlight down on the shelf with immaculate care and slid her finger under the curved hook of a hanger bearing a small red coat. Inch by inch, she drew it towards her.

Before turning to the exit, she glanced towards the back of the store and saw a row of down jackets in adult sizes. She looked at the exit, then back at the jackets, and after pausing for a moment to assess the silence, walked towards them. The first pine green coat on the rack was exactly her size.

As she pulled the hangar towards her, it clinked on the end of the rail. The hanger spilled over her finger and sailed down to the floor, pinging the concrete once, twice, three times. The woman gasped, and her eyes widened into molten orbs of fear.

Just beyond her, a faint clicking sound emerged from the silence. Not loud, not sharp, just a series of taps in quick succession. Her eyes snapped towards the direction of the clicking, a set of massive shelves housing car top skiing boxes. The boxes lay almost tomb-like, long and black and covered in dust, their lack of utility in this world as much a factor of their deadness as their physical inanimacy. She squinted at their seams, their corners. The clicking persisted, louder now, more of a rattle, and one of the car top boxes began to move. It seemed to almost come apart, a long appendage extending from the shell all the way to the floor, clicking incessantly. Another appendage descended from the box, and then two more, until all four hellish feet of an invader camouflaged in the shelves stood before her. From the same shelf, two more chameleonic invaders unfurled, and as they dropped to the ground, their bodies morphed from black to trademark maroon.

Like a choir of demons, all three screeched in unison. Their calls were swiftly answered by identical screeches on the first floor. Another screech, and then another. They were all over the place.

Something left the woman when the distant churning of the pickup's engine found her ears — that chug, chug, chug, chug, vroom. There were screeches in the lot now.

"Oh, God."

Almost as if the invaders knew, as if they wanted her to hear it, all their hellish screeching paused just long enough for the blunted crunch of a vehicle collision in the parking lot to reach the woman's ears.

"Oh, no. No. No!"

One of the three invaders before her leapt in a perfectly vertical motion through a hole in the roof. Another one followed. The third sprang back and bound straight past the woman and down the escalator.

She threw down the coat and ran out of the store, tearing her pants on the chain link security door. Two more invaders were ahead of her, galloping down the escalator, and three more emerged from other stores on the second floor.

Pivoting on her front foot, she spun and fired a single round at the group behind her, the bullet tearing into the mouth lining of the one in front. The invader seized and stumbled, tripping the two behind it so that all three became a barreling avalanche of limbs and rage and noise.

The few seconds it took them to gather themselves afforded the woman enough time to bound down the escalator to the mall entrance. The sapling that had been there now lay in shambles halfway across the lot.

The pickup sat dead with its front end crunched up against the concrete base of a light pole. The windshield was gone, a plume of black smoke piped from the engine. One invader was working to rip the cabin off from the chassis while three more pecked at something on the asphalt several yards away. That something was the bleeding heap of the girl, fingers of a severed left forearm still gripped around her slingshot.

The woman stood statue-still next to the broken sapling, boiling and breaking and so utterly arrested, helplessly watching invaders tear the girl's corpse apart. She reversed her grip on the hunting rifle and lowered her converter.

The air she inhaled was clean, pure, almost life-giving. She held her breath for a moment, letting it fill every crevice of her lungs. When she exhaled, she put the muzzle of the hunting rifle in her mouth, its frigid metal clinking along her teeth.

Two invaders still in the mall burst into the parking lot, and one of them crashed into the woman, jamming the rifle into her throat and knocking out two of her back molars with a chalky snap.

She cried out in pain as the hunting rifle clattered to the asphalt and the invader spun on top of her. Reaching back, she propped herself on her elbows and grabbed the butt of the gun. The invader readied a great claw, a lanky and mangled web of blades, and it swung down just as the woman scooched forward far enough to evade it. She crawled out to face the invader, and when it turned and screeched, she speared its mouth with the muzzle and fired a round right down its throat. A horizontal geyser of blood spewed forth, coating the woman's entire face and torso, a mix of matter from human and monster gliding down her throbbing jaw. She spat out her two molars amongst the phlegm.

The invader galloped away screeching but fell limp in the shallow of the hills behind the mall. Silence fell over the lot. The rest of the invaders were gone. There was no wind, no movement. The woman was alone.

With one hand on her jaw and the other gripping the barrel of the rifle, the woman turned around. She began pacing towards a red heap glistening by the truck. Whatever blood from the invader hadn't dried on her dripped in a dark wake.

When the woman reached what was left of the girl, she knelt. She ran her eyes over everything that still looked like a human and everything that didn't, every tear and tatter and limb and clump of hair.

A screech rose from far off in the hills, and an invader broke into a canter towards the mall. The woman slowly took the slingshot from the girl's hand and put it in her pocket. Then she took the girl's forearm and strode over to the truck. She placed it in a bed of shattered glass on the passenger seat.

She started the engine. After a series of chugs and wheezes, it reluctantly turned over, and the woman threw it into reverse and stomped on the gas. The tires squealed as she peeled out of the parking lot, invader in slow pursuit behind her.

The next few days came to her more so as a dream than as reality.

She ran. Not just from invaders, but from the world, from herself, and from the few tethers to her soul she had remaining. She did not eat, she did not sleep. She ran, and she watched, and she worried. She buried the girl's forearm somewhere on the cabin's property but soon forgot where. She sat in silence looking at her hands, hands that never stopped bleeding, not even at night, and she gave quarter to ghostly voices rising in the fields. She saw cruel shapes dance about the forest, specters mixed of form and void, soft and speckled nether beings that an ancient part of her knew were always there yet never saw. But now she saw them, and they saw her, and she retreated into them and made them her home.

She drove the pickup all the way out to the campground where evil's heavy footsteps still lurked, and under the cover of a faultless fall evening in the valley, found the purple pouch. She cradled the dirty canvas object in her hands before unceremoniously opening its draw-string and dropping in a bead with a Mickey Mouse sticker and two worn down crayons, one black and one red.

After she moved the fuel crate from the pickup to the van that had months ago brought her here — its windows gone, its tires flat, its panels riddled with bullet holes — she drove it on the rims to the service road in the desert where she had been left to die. Her bike was still there behind the boulder. She spent many days fixing it and many nights speaking with things in the cold, blue wild.

"I'm rotten," she said, her voice almost an animal's.

When the bike finally ran again, she fueled it and turned her back on a dry winter morning.

And while riding some days later, the chrome shimmer of a toppled chopper in a narrow clearing of switchgrass caught her eye.

She pulled over and examined it. The wind was strong that day, unforgiving.

Gaff's decaying body laid some feet away in a pool of weeds.

She took a step back and stared at what was left of him as if it was some science experiment. His eyes were gone. His flesh was sun-dried and pecked over — vulture food — and his skeletal mouth lay wrenched open in permanent terror.

El Diablo had found him.

In the shadow of a pale blue dawn, the woman gathered straw, brittle brown wisps sucked of their life and their softness by the onset of winter. She mumbled to herself through chapped lips, emitting words and syllables that glommed together like a cold residue in her converter. She looked up and cursed a disk that was not there.

A piercing wind blew in from across the river. It swept several stalks out of her hand and cut against the inset of her cheeks — one still two molars short of the other. She cursed again.

Meager bolts of straw lodged in her fists, she shuffled over the hardening dirt to the cabin. Without so much as a glance, she passed the vegetable garden, now a graveyard of twisted brown compost that lay tentacled over empty water jugs, pale white eggs half-swallowed up by the earth. Gone were the wreaths and garlands of wildflowers draping the cabin's exterior. She had removed them. Now, nothing masked the rot expanding across its splintered wooden timbers.

She shivered as she opened the door, and with a scornful glare, cast a darkness through the place that hadn't been there before she entered. Everything she did was shrouded in that darkness — her words, her thoughts, her movements. On the kitchen counter, a handful of shriveled mushrooms sat in a small bowl. She snatched a few of them, lowered her converter, and chomped them down.

She hand-jammed the straw into the arm of a shirt that was nearly stuffed — a child's shirt, a little girl's — attached to a girl's pair of pants. For a head, the woman had placed a clay jug upside down and smeared mud and chalk across it to form a face. The doll's hair — bits of string and twine pulled from all manner of places dirty and forgotten — sprouted wildly, making the thing look like some kind of eccentric porcupine. The woman stepped back and looked at the doll, leered at it. Then she cupped a hand to its cheek.

"My Constance. Is that you?"

Constance was seated on the floor next to the fireplace. Bryce sat at the table. He was constructed in much the same way, old clothes stuffed with straw and scrap, twigs busting from appendage holes, garish features scrawled onto a muddy jug of a head. Small green eyeglasses.

"Isn't it good to see your younger sister again?" the woman said, turning to Bryce.

Bryce said nothing.

"I said, isn't it good to see your sister again? Don't start playing this game with me. She's been gone for a long time but I've found her again. Just like I found you."

She stared at the doll for a long time. Gusts of wind careened through the cabin's wood panels and swept loose straw across the floor.

"I'm only going to ask nicely one more time. Isn't it good to see your sister again? I told you I was going to bring her back. Don't be shy, now."

"Yes, mom," said Bryce.

"Thank you." She went back to work on Constance, smoothing her hair and adjusting the lumps in her clothing. On the mantle above the fireplace, she had lined up the rest of the items she kept in the purple pouch — the Mickey Mouse bead, the red and black crayons, the dog collar, the action figure, Elijah's picture. The wedding band was on her finger. It clanked against her bulbous knuckles like a solitary bead on an abacus wire. As for the pouch itself, it too was stuffed with straw, and the woman cradled it in both hands and began cooing to it. She sang to it. She rocked it in her arms and smiled under her converter.

"My angel. My most perfect one. You returned to me."

Outside, the world was calm, a fluorescent moon glowing mightily. The river quieted, ice hardening along its edges, and the pomp and circumstance of evening insects chilled down to a winter's murmur.

The woman sat at the table with Bryce and Constance on either side of her, the baby in a highchair she'd constructed from pieces of the shed out back.

"Something's been bothering me," said Constance.

They sat under the light of a single candle, each with sticks of magpie jerky and oddly shaped pickled vegetables on plates that didn't match.

"I haven't had a new pair of ballet shoes since I was eight and I'm afraid they'll mess me up in tryouts. Bryce gets new football cleats every year."

"That's because I'm going to high school next year," said Bryce. "My sports are serious. Yours aren't."

"Yes, huh!" said Constance.

The woman glared at her. "Don't raise your voice. You'll upset your baby sister."

"But Bryce always acts like he's more important!"

"You'll get your ballet shoes this year, and Bryce will get his cleats. We've had such a good harvest this year. We were able to get by most of the month on my disability check."

The woman didn't eat what was on hers or any of the plates. She walked over to the baby and cradled it in her arms, arms that had shrunk in recent weeks to long rails of flesh sagging away from the bone. She cooed to the baby through her converter.

The next day, she instructed Constance to watch the baby while she and Bryce went out. "I've got two bottles in the fridge for her," she said, lashing Bryce to her backpack. "We should be back by the time you need to give her the second one."

"So, do I give her the second one or not?" Constance said.

"If we get back before dark, no. If it gets dark and she gets hungry, yes."

With Bryce swinging from her back, his odd head poking above hers like part of some pagan costume, she set out along a mountain path half-obscured by eroding autumn leaves. Every so often, they'd pass a sturdy oak with a rectangle blaze painted on its trunk. The blazes were so weathered that their colors were no longer clear, the blues and yellows and reds all smudging into the hard contours of the bark. A pair of rabbits darted across the trail several yards ahead, but rather than move to hunt them, the woman kept her eyes glued to the trees. She pointed at a group of aspens.

"Remember those trees? What are they called?" she said.

"Aspens."

"Do you remember what makes aspens special?"

"They're connected underground by their roots. Many trees, one being."

She smiled and picked up her pace. "Good job, Bryce. Very good."

She scavenged the fields for grasses of a certain fragrance, snapping them at the root and sniffing the broken ends like a feral animal. The mushrooms were identifiable on sight alone. She gathered many of both such plants and stuffed them ungroomed and unbagged into the backpack to which the mannequin of her son was tied.

Late in the day, she took a pumice from the bag and gnashed a few of the grasses and mushrooms into a slimy brown paste, and she took off her converter and smeared the stuff along her gums, her tongue, and the roof of her mouth.

At evening's call, she started back down the trail towards the cabin, but was compelled elsewhere by a murky black object drifting high above the mountains. Too small to be a disk, too dark to be a star, it loped in a leisurely fashion like a tadpole through a pond, and although the woman did not recognize it for what it was, she sat there and watched it all the way to its point of dissipation in the broad distant north.

She regaled Bryce with stories about the stars when they quelled the day's last red rim of sunlight, weaving intoxicated narrative threads into an odd quilt of astrological speculations and half-truths. But the stars faded, and the black blackened, and she camped uncovered on the edge of the forest where the trunks of the aspens jutted out of the immeasurable night like rail thin ghosts advancing upon her. Save for their shimmer, she laid there with her head on her pack in a state of darkness entire.

Many shades and shadows sensed her and tiptoed from their dwellings in the trees, the lakes, the black peppercorn hills. They followed her home to the cabin in the morning, and in the days and weeks after, claimed new dwellings in proximity to the darkness in her heart. She spent time talking with them and with her children. Not sleeping and not eating, scuttling about the cabin and its surrounding lands.

One night, she sensed something staring at her from across the river. Gripping the waistline of her trousers to keep them on, she grabbed the binoculars and climbed to the roof.

To the unaided eye, it was a shiny black speck hanging in the pocket between two mountains. When she gazed at it through the binoculars, it was a vaguely shaped oval made of a black that nearly blinded her. It held a dark so deep, so absolute, that the object was devoid of any color, as if a cosmic needle had punctured a hole in the earth's firmament.

"Get the fuck off me, shade. I did not invite you here. I made no bargain."

"But bargains I can offer," it said, "avenues to ease your pain. All I would seek in return is to move a bit closer."

She threw down the binoculars and cursed the speck, but it hung there in the pocket each night thereafter. It did not move closer, but its presence in the woman's mind grew until one night it could grow no more.

Something lingering in her room woke her. Not a sight but a feeling, a presence standing in the doorway. The woman was naked, and she sat up in bed in her silence and her smallness.

The human objects in the room with her were cold, stiff. They were blank relics from another time and place, things suffocating under blankets of dust and locked in the attic of a forgotten civilization. Here, lost in the vastness of her isolation — crushed under the sheer weight of it — the woman herself had become a relic.

With weary eyes, red and crusted with day-old mucus, she looked at the doorway. Nothing there. She turned to regard the speck through the single pane window, and then she looked up at the moon. It loomed large in the sky, a celestial strobe light waxing gibbous over snow-capped mountains. Its light coated the land in a smooth, silver glow as flakes drifted down from the heavens.

"Mom?"

Constance's voice from the doorway was gentle, a coaxing whisper. As soft as the falling snow outside, she stepped around the bed and sat next to her mother. "Are you okay?"

The woman didn't respond. She didn't move. "You're not real, sweetie."

Constance placed two cold fingers over the scar where the invader's claw had sliced into her mother's quad. "Does it still hurt?"

The woman closed her eyes. "No."

Constance peeked around her mother's shoulder, her eyes landing on a thin line etched over two bulging neck vertebrae. "How did you get that one?"

"That was from spine surgery. I was in a bad car accident right after Bryce was born."

She put a hand on a portion of her mother's lower back, where the skin was uneven, almost thatched. "What about this? That's a big one."

"That was from a burn. That one hurt a lot."

"What happened?"

"It was during my first overseas deployment. Another time when the world was hurting. I don't want to talk about it."

She scanned her mother's entire body. She saw everything, inside and out. She was quiet for a long time, and then she cried. "You have so many. Are you sure they don't hurt?"

The woman's breath hitched as she conjured her neck into a series of jilted nods. Her entire body was heavy and stiff, her limbs like lumps of concrete, the pain in her hips and her back throbbing. She shut her eyes tightly, blinking away tears.

Constance snaked a forearm under her mother's and leaned into her. They clasped hands, and the woman let herself fall into her daughter. The girl was cold, colder than the dead winter's night. "All of those things are so far away from you now. You've had enough pain." Her voice grew darker, less human. "Come home, mom. We're all waiting for you."

Sometime later, when Constance had departed and the woman released herself to sleep, she was with them again in a bright white place. She felt them more than she saw them, blurry blotches surrounded by shimmering light, like flowy linen dresses billowing in the wind. They didn't speak because they didn't need to. In this place, everything had already been said. Everything had already been felt. Even time was not necessary. Now, there was just this: release.

The smile that had worked itself across the woman's face in dream was still there when the light of a country dawn woke her, and it was still there — scrunched under her converter — when she set out in the morning.

Rope in hand, she trudged into the forest.

She passed through reefs of winter snow stirred up by the wind, under thick-plated pine boughs fat with sap. Old rocks — brown, black, and gray — shone under fresh snowmelt, and they lined the banks of streams that cut through the hills like ice water veins. She followed one of the streams up a mountain ledge to the crest of a head-height esker, and throwing the rope above, gripped the rock with both hands and scampered up.

She trekked on. A darker noon saw her up ledges steeper yet, like an insect creeping toward some cryptic light. In the afternoon, she emerged over the tree line through a region bald and faultless, where the looming shadows of peaks knifed through the placid white yonder, and the tracks she left in the snow stood out as spotted violations of these upper reaches where gods dwelt more than men.

Chains of lightning split through skies pregnant with rain, the skyline's heightened ridges melting upward like the dark atmosphere of a distant planet governed not by gravity, but by fear. Accompanying thunder clapped from the north and filled the basins around her, smooth and rumbling rolls, great growls from an ill titan squirming in some unfathomable turmoil. So dark and terrible were the clouds that their very color seemed to suggest a more sinister intent.

When at last she reached the spot — a narrow cliff hanging off the blunt edge of a mountain — the storms had rolled further west towards the coast, and a circle of stars unfurled in the cool blue dusk.

She took off her converter as she looked up at them, the smile on her fissured face bending in a wide arc. She tied one end of the rope around a boulder at the top of the ledge, sat on the ledge so that her feet dangled over, and slipped the noose end around her neck.

For a long moment she sat there, hands folded, feet still, eyes fixed on the night sky and those that dwelt in it. Despite the cold, a fire in her chest warmed her, stirring her to emotion as it melted down walls she'd built around vast archives of memories, moments that had long ago brought her joy. She looked at the stars and smiled.

"Hi," she said to them. Her voice was soft and strained. "Hi guys. I'm coming. I'm coming home."

She peered out at the land, that vast expanse of earth and tree, of snow and rock and cold and light.

She chuckled, tears rolling down her dirty cheeks. "You know what, though? I didn't let those fuckers get me, did I? Eleven years. Eleven years I didn't let them get me. I don't know why, but this whole time I knew they wouldn't. I was never afraid of them because I knew they couldn't... I knew they couldn't hurt me anymore than they did when they took you. In the end, I guess it was you. Wasn't it? I just can't be here anymore without you. I tried to tell you. I tried so many times. I know you can hear me. I... I hope you can hear me. I really hope you're there."

She sighed and looked at her hands. The blood on them had dried.

"Okay," she whispered, nodding. "Okay."

She closed her eyes, and with one swift push, lifted her body off the ledge.

When the rope snapped taut, the noose wrenched around her neck, smashing her larynx and strangling the arteries around it. She coughed, hacked, kicked her legs.

But just as the colors around her collapsed into a cackling black centroid of sheer extinguishment, a shiny blue object at the bottom of the ledge caught her eye.

It was her husband.

He had descended. He had come down from the mountains where he roamed without her, and now he was standing some handful of yards below her in the snow.

He was exactly how she remembered him, except this time, more vivid and real. So real. Tall, sturdy, hair closely cropped. The silver stars on each of his shoulders glinted in the moonlight, and the dark blue uniform fitted tightly to his body may have been made of the night itself. His face was grave, focused, commanding. He was staring right at her, straight through to her soul. It had been so long since she'd seen those eyes — really seen them. And when he spoke to her, his voice carried the weight of a hundred thunder filled basins.

"Come down from there," he said.

The woman stabbed her fingers through the noose, clawing wildly for millimeters of space between the rope and her neck. Her legs whipped back and forth, and she swung her body to try to reach the cliff wall. She tried to call his name, but her voice didn't work.

The life was almost out of her when, on the comeback of a longer swing, the rope slipped off the rock above, and the woman, noose still tied on, fell flailing to the ground. She fell for several seconds and landed on her back in a diagonal snowbank, mere feet from where her husband had been standing. She laid there hacking and gasping for life. When she finally loosened the noose enough to breathe, she laid there hyperventilating for some time in the frigid snow.

When she sat up, her husband was gone.

"Jason?" she said, still coughing. "Jason!"

She twisted to view the rock that held the noose, and the iridescent eyes of a raven glared back at her. The bird was utterly massive, maybe half the size of a child. It was as if the weight of her husband's voice had found itself in the strength of the raven's eyes, gold-rimmed jewels raging with ancient flame.

"Is it you?" she said to the raven.

The raven hoisted itself off the rock and spread its wings, black sheets of night dipped in a mystic blue glow. With heavy flaps that whooshed in the night, it coasted down the mountain and disappeared beyond the tree line.

Hands still clutching the noose around her neck, the woman fell to her knees and wept.

"You can't do this to me!" Her lungs had conjured the strength of a scream, but all that came out was a cracked whisper. "I can't do this anymore!"

She spent a long time crying and freezing and looking up at the stars before finally slipping the noose off her head. Elbows on her knees and face in her hands, she shook her head, refusing to accept her inherent truth.

"I have nothing left, Jason. What am I supposed to do? I'm just so lost. Tell me what I'm supposed to do."

The morning offered tepid warmth as she made her way back down the mountain. She first returned to the ledge to retrieve her converter and looked down at the scuffle her landing had made below. Before leaving, she washed handfuls of snow over her face and hands.

The sky was cloudless, and the snowbanks glistened under a hard yellow sun, and the tips of trees and edges of rocks twinkled as she passed them by. She came upon a group of birds pecking at the ground in a snow-melted meadow, a dozen magpies and a single raven that seemed to serve as suzerain of the group. The woman's presence didn't stir them, and although her stomach cried out in hunger, she paid them no mind having no tool to hunt with. Her eyes were glued to the treetops, darting through the high branches where an owl might dwell.

Down at the cabin, a green van was parked next to the garden. The sight of it arrested her, but she gathered herself and resumed her trek when the door to the cabin creaked open and Regis stepped out. He waved to her, and the warmth of his smile was unmarred by a mouth of half-rotten teeth.

"Where's your converter?" she said through hers.

His smile remained as he extended his hands. "They're gone."

"What?"

"Look up at that sky. Not a disk in sight!"

She looked up, using a hand to shield her eyes from the sun. "Really?"

"When was the last time you saw a disk?"

"I'm guess I'm not sure. They really gone?"

"As far as we know, yes. The disks are all gone."

She lowered her hand and looked at him quizzically.

"There are still some invaders out there but they don't attack anymore. It's kinda odd, really. It's like they lost their power or desire to kill when the disks left."

They embraced when she reached the cabin. Regis did poorly to mask his stare at the red burn around the woman's neck.

"Somebody once told me there were different beings inside the disks, like living computers. Maybe they controlled the invaders."

"Maybe so," Regis said. "Who knows? The sight of 'em, though, still strikes fear into the soul. I don't think that'll ever change. People hundreds of years from now will have nightmares about them."

The woman slid her index fingers under the straps of her converter, but stopped and glared at Regis.

He nodded. "Go ahead. It'll feel good."

"How are you sure?"

"I guess you'll just have to trust me."

She sighed. "Well, if you're not gonna wear yours, it won't be much good for me to wear mine."

Regis chuckled as she took the machine away from her face. "It's good to see you again, old friend."

"How did you know I was here?"

"You told me, remember?"

"Yeah, but how did you know I was here right now?"

"Well, you weren't when I got here last night, but I saw the bike and figured it would just be a matter of time. He wrapped a gloved hand around one of the bike's handles. "How's this old girl holding up?"

"Okay, I suppose. Big thing it needs is a fork alignment. Needed that for a while. Some tire rot, too."

"I see that."

"Brake pads probably need to be replaced. Just the normal stuff."

"How's the electrical?"

"Fine. I rewired a lot of it recently. Cleaned the engine and the ignition system. Could always be better. I'm no electrician."

"You have the new pads?"

"I actually do."

"No seat cover. What, you like sitting on sharp metal slats?"

"They're impossible to find."

He took his hand off the bike and looked around. "Where's that girl you had with you last time?"

She dug her hands into the saddlebags and retrieved a blue cardboard box. She held it up. "Got the brake pads right here."

Regis nodded, and he folded his hands under his belly the way a monk might as he gazed at her. "Is she here?"

The woman put the box back in the saddlebags. "I dropped her off at 219. She has some family there. I visit her from time to time. It's for the best. It's a better life."

Regis nodded. "I've got something for you inside. Want to see it?"

"Do I have a choice?"

He chuckled and opened the door.

A fire had been lit, a pot strung up above it. In the corner, a sleeping bag had been unfurled against the wall. A small cooler was nearby. Regis sighed as he crouched in front of the hearth, his knees cracking. He lifted the pot by the handle, took two mugs off a shelf, and smiled as he poured steaming coffee into each of them.

"My God," she said. "I haven't smelled that in years."

"I'm not done yet," he said, eyes shining.

He opened the cooler and took out a bottle of milk.

"Where on earth did you get that? Is that real?"

"Realer than you'll ever know."

He poured a splash into one of the mugs and looked at her. "Want some?"

"Where did it come from? Like, what creature produced that?"

"Use your head."

She recoiled. "Is that breast milk?"

"Filtered and pasteurized."

"Regis. Gross."

"Is it? A couple women started a business in the comm and they're doing great for themselves. It's a hot commodity. Or, I guess, a lukewarm commodity."

"Ugh."

"Hey, don't act like you're above it."

The woman sat at the table and shook her head. "Fine."

He finished pouring and sat across from her. The woman looked at the dolls of Bryce and Constance seated in the other two chairs. She took a sip and closed her eyes, licked her chapped lips.

"Whatcha think?" Regis said.

"It's good. It's actually really good."

After the woman ate some vegetables, they spent a brisk and overcast day working on the bike.

Regis found some rebar in the shed and bent it with two pairs of pliers into a seat frame. He covered the rebar with sheet metal, braced it with scraps of wood, bolted on the original hinges from the saddle, and threaded a tight weave of tie wire through the lid to make a latch for the lock.

He snapped it into place just as the woman started the brake pad installation. She removed the calipers, scrubbed them down with an old toothbrush, dried them, put the pistons back in, dressed the rotor, and snapped in the pads.

"Where'd that eight-millimeter go?" she said.

"Hold on, I've got the ten in there." Regis wiped the grease off a wrench and swapped a larger socket for a smaller one, handed it to her.

She attached the caliper, and wrench in hand, torqued the fasteners.

He pumped the brake lever and checked the fluid level. "Wanna bleed 'em?"

"You don't have any brake fluid, do you?"

"Oh, how you doubt me." Regis went to his van and retrieved a canister of brake fluid. He removed the cap and the diaphragm and prepped the bleed nipple on the caliper, then knelt and carefully poured a small amount of fluid into the reservoir. The woman stood over the bike and pumped on the brakes as Regis opened and closed the bleeder bolt on the caliper. Dark liquid snaked through the hose and into a vial suffocating in his meathook of a hand. Once they repeated the process several times, Regis stepped back and looked at his work.

"Wanna test her?" she said, handing him the keys.

"That's all you. How about you test it and I'll make us some dinner?"

"You sure? You don't have to do all this."

Regis was already on his way to the door. "We'll fix that alignment tomorrow. It's too cold out here for me, anyway."

The woman rubbed a hand over the new seat he had made and tested the lock. "Damn, Regis. Nice."

She started the bike and flicked on the halogen. It shot a beam out into the chalky black distance, into a mist-laden glade of indeterminate size where the things that haunted her roamed. But tonight, they did not. Tonight, she was whole, and she drove the bike through spaces knowable only to those who dared to venture into them. Out there, she guided her new brakes through the discovery of their limitations, tapping them at various speeds in the sharp winter wind.

Something flickered off-road in the darkness.

The woman slowed the bike and guided the halogen towards the disturbance, and she put her hand to her mouth to feel for a converter that was not there. The halogen landed on two hunched-over invaders out in a meadow. Their crimson plating was covered in large white blotches, and they moved like waifs, strung out and listless by the ashy ruins of another cabin. The hum of the bike's motor did not distract them, and they seemed not to notice the halogen shining in their faces. A strong gust of wind toppled one of them over. The other opened its mouth to moan.

The woman squinted at them. She tightened the grip on her handlebars and swallowed the lump in her throat, and after watching them struggle for a moment longer, drove softly away.

When she parked the bike and approached the cabin, its windows glowed gold from the light of a well-tended fire. She smiled as she reached for the door, but the midnight croaks of a raven high froze her dead in her tracks and ran a blade across her heart. Her knees buckled.

She darted around to the other side of the cabin, but no eyes and no creature were there to meet her. All that moved were ripples on the river that shimmered like tinsel in the boldface light of a full moon. She winced in physical pain, planted her back against the cabin, and slid down to the ground slowly. She put her head in her hands, and she stayed there for some time, wheezing and suppressing screams and peering out over the trees. "Okay," she said, gathering herself. "Okay."

Inside, Regis had prepared tea and some kind of porridge. He turned to look at the woman when she entered.

"Leveled her out?" he said.

"Yeah. I can't thank you enough." She peeled off her boots with a series of grunts and sat down at the table. "And that seat? It even locks. I never could have done that."

He placed a bowl down in front of her, then one in front of himself.

"Saw two of 'em out in the meadow there," she said in between slurps. "I see what you mean."

"Were they red or white?"

"It looked like they were turning white or stained white, or something."

"Seems to be their way of dying of natural causes. We're not really sure."

The woman shook her head. "Crazy."

The dolls of Bryce and Constance were still in their chairs. Regis looked at Bryce, then at Constance.

"I know. It's ridiculous," she said.

"What?"

"Them. I just got kinda lonely. That's all."

Regis nodded. "Aren't you gonna introduce me?"

"Please. Don't patronize me."

"I'm serious. Who are they?"

The woman got up and placed another log on the fire. She looked down at Regis from across the room. "If you really want to know, they're my kids. I'm able to spend time with them, in a way."

Regis took the woman's empty bowl and refilled it with porridge, almost to the brim. He set it down in front of her as she sat back down.

The woman didn't respond, just looked down at her bowl and resumed eating.

"So, listen." Regis put his hands on the table in a presentational manner. "Things have changed at 445 since the invaders left. For the better. We're able to come and go to the depots as we please, and because of our geography, people are flocking to us for transportation. We're taking the walls down in the spring. There are a lot of good people trying to move across the western flank right now, a lot of folks trying to get east."

The woman maintained her focus on the porridge.

"Bottom line is, we're building a motor pool at the comm, and I need good help. We're going to provide repairs, guarded transportation, message delivery, the works. I know you like being on your own and I respect that, but I can't help but wonder if you might want to stay with us on a permanent basis." He put his hand around Bryce's straw-filled cuff but kept his eyes on the woman. "If you don't mind me saying so, I think it would do you some good."

She took a long beat before answering, her gaze stony and her head cocked down away from her guest. "I'm not sure I'm ready for something like that."

"Why don't you at least think about it? You wouldn't need to live there necessarily. I'm just..." His words trailed off as his chin fell to his chest. He took his hand away from the doll. "I'm a little worried about you. I'm afraid you might have forgotten that there are people who still care about you. Plus, we could really use someone with your skills. That's all."

She glanced around the cabin. The table, the fire, the doors, the windows. Bryce, Constance. The dog collar on the mantle. "This was a very good meal, Regis. Thank you." She scooched back her chair. "I'm gonna bed down."

With his index fingers, Regis drew the woman's bowl towards him and stacked it under his. "Brought you some more blankets. You were looking a little sparse in there. They're on the bed."

She stopped in the bedroom doorway, half turned to him, nodded, and disappeared into the darkness.

Warmed under a mound of blankets and a hot meal in her stomach, the woman slept dreamlessly through the morning and into the afternoon. The clang of pounding metals woke her.

She sat up in bed and cracked her neck, sighing. A fog off the river had crept up shore to cloak the cabin and surrounding land.

Out the window, Regis stood on the foot pegs of the bike, and with his hands on the handlebars, thrust his weight down over the entire front end. As if performing a kind of mechanical CPR, over and over he slammed down through the front suspension, metal snapping with each thrust. He was a vague and ethereal creature out there in the mist, his movements resembling a ghost's more than a man's.

Shoulders draped in blankets and skin leathery from rest, the woman opened the cabin door. "Mornin'"

Regis picked up a socket wrench and snapped a socket onto the drive square. "Afternoon. You slept good."

"Too good."

"Nah, you needed it." He started torquing a bolt on the yoke.

"You breaking my bike out here?"

He chuckled. "Aligned your fork, dummy. Now wake up and help me tack the fender back on."

She took slight steps over to the front of the bike, her bare feet gathering a coat of chilly condensation. She smiled.

Regis put the wrench down and turned to give her a good look. "I haven't seen you smile like that in a long time. You're practically grinning."

"You're the best, Regis."

"Wheel shouldn't cheat left on you now." He stood and handed her a second wrench, ratchet end out for her to grasp it. "Wanna help? Fender's not gonna reattach itself."

She turned away from him, keeping her hands under the blanket. "You're doing good. Don't let me get in your way."

"Hey!" As if it was a divining stick, the wrench still in Regis' hand traced her movement back to the cabin. His jaw fell open. "What?"

"I'll make us some breakfast."

"I already had breakfast. It's time for lunch."

The woman was already at the door. "It's veggies and jerky either way."

"Hell, it's almost dinnertime!"

The door closed. Regis wiped his brow with a rag from his back pocket.

They spent the next four days cohabitating in this manner, working and talking and eating together. With the woman's bike running better than it had in years, they turned to Regis' van. They were able to raise it a good foot off the ground with a pair of jacks, high enough for the woman to slip underneath. Regis pulled off all four tires, and the woman replaced the ball joints. The next day, they popped the hood and wiped down everything they could reach — the engine, the filters, the ignition system, the battery and its terminals. They removed the starter, the alternator, and the radiator, and they cleaned those too before putting everything back, save for the starter, which Regis suggested they altogether replace. He already had the new part on him. He gave it to the woman, and she installed it, her smaller hands much nimbler in that claustrophobic jungle of iron and steel.

They washed their hands and faces in the river, and in the fading daylight, cracked through the ice and caught a perch with a makeshift ice fishing rig. The woman cooked it over the fireplace, fileted and seasoned it, and Regis made them a hot tea flavored with lemon and pepper. "This'll clear your sinuses right out," he said.

In the morning, they rose from their separate rooms and set off with a pair of axes and a bandsaw from the shed. They walked to the edge of the forest and the woman laid a hand on the trunk of a ponderosa pine. She peered up into its branches. "This one."

Gripping opposite ends of the bandsaw, they dug its rusty teeth into the bark and eased it back and forth. It took them twenty minutes to get halfway, and an hour to cut through the rest. The tree fell back against its fellow pines on the edge of the forest, sending needles flying over an area of what seemed like miles. The woman stared at the stump's newly exposed rings, those hard-earned centuries of growth, as scents of bark and sap filled her nostrils. The scent was pure, and it was good. She touched a hand to her face to verify she wore no converter.

Then they took turns whacking down a single severance point

on up the fallen log, the two of them moving in smooth rhythm, one slamming a downswing while the other coiled an upswing, down through the meat of the pine until it broke apart. All the while, a bright winter sun shone through the naked tips of trees and warmed the earth. At one point, Regis threw down his coat. He asked to sit for a few moments, and she followed suit. The woman stared at his hunched and labored body and saw the age in it. She sat on the toppled log and turned the wooden ax handle in her hands, pressing it against her calluses and massaging it in her fingers. Her hands were clean, her grip was strong, and realizing the blood that had stained them was gone, pulled her gaze above the cabin and out over the river. The black speck wasn't there. In the pocket of the mountains, a faultless wedge of azure sky.

Twice more, they divided the fallen log with dueling swings, and then they used the stump they'd created as the base to split the four logs into firewood. Dusk had arrived by the time they'd ported all the wood back to the cabin, stacking it against the outside wall under the water pump. Regis grabbed a tarp from the van. Both of them moved with the stiffness of fatigue from a long day of lumberjacking in the cold.

"I need to see about getting back to the comm," Regis said, tossing one end of the rustling tarp over the woodpile. "Was planning to head out tomorrow unless you need me for anything else."

The woman kept head down, eyes focused on her end of the tarp. She ran the hook of a fraying bungee cord through the grommet and pulled it taut. "Sure, that's fine."

He walked around the pile and stood over her. "Come with me. There's a life for you there."

"There's a life for me here."

He stood his ax knob down and leaned on it, then sat. "Those ligature marks on your neck tell me otherwise."

Her hands stopped working. She glared at him.

"Already told you once, this world is better with you in it." He looked at her for a long while, the night settling in around them. "My world is better with you in it."

The woman stood. "I'd appreciate your help with one last thing before you go."

Regis nodded. With a groan, he heaved himself up and ambled into the cabin.

The woman stayed outside and looked to the south, where stars aplenty dazzled around a metallic half-moon. She stood there and carried a wordless conversation, her breath clouds fogging the stars over in pulses, and then clearing. At one point, she nodded and said, "All right."

Regis pointed to the meal he had made for her on the table when she entered the cabin. He had already nestled into his sleeping bag by the fire, a book in his weathered hands and a smile across his face. She ate, and they said little, and when she retreated to her bedroom, she packed a pipe and smoked until her eyes were weary enough for rest.

So much time had passed since those early nights, but the woman found herself back at the karaoke bar with a microphone in one hand and a drink in the other. She struggled to keep up with the words and had long abandoned staying in tune. A dozen faces in the loud little room stared back at her, cawing and singing in the blinking green light. From the crowd, the eyes of her future husband seized her through a young man's sockets. That penetrating gaze was the kindling for a fire that sparked her womb — something she'd never felt before — and she stared back at him with the hunger of a young woman sensing her future fall into place. He emerged through the crowd and led her out of the room.

When they stepped through the door together, they were deep into the gorges. There were towering red rock faces, white tracks of sandstone, fissures of immense depth, trees that flowered indigo and lavender. There was a steep yellow mountain, curved and poking through the sky, and there were bends of a river crimped around mesas and weaving clear across the earth. She followed him into a slot canyon where the rock walls were cool and dark. He turned around and put his hands on her, and she draped her forearms over his shoulders. She wrapped her legs around his waist as he pinned her up against the rock, its sharp chill splashing her skin and fueling the ecstasy inside her. Their soft moans echoed through the desert.

The next morning came late. It was foggy again, and the temperature had plummeted to depths enough to cool the blood of even the warmest of creatures. They bundled themselves in the first gray light and struck out like a pair of pioneers drifting across a cloud-clogged nowhere.

She led them north along the river as it snaked around field and dale, and then she steered them through a meadow that grew rockier with distance. Above them, tree branches hung somehow closer to the ground, and the white spaces between their trunks seemed to glow. One such tree — an old dead pine, a wild-looking assortment of sharp angles and ivory knives stabbing those that would approach it — marked a turnoff that led to a waist high wrought-iron gate. A rusting and forgotten construction, it creaked as the woman nudged it open with the toe of her boot. She stepped into the graveyard and Regis followed.

Most of the stones lay chipped or leaning or covered in moss, even the newer ones. Older stone faces had melted over time, all but erasing the glyphs that served as their occupants' last frayed connection to the earth. In the very back corner of the place, edges of a white, uncut quartz beamed up from the leaves. Not taking her eyes off the stone, the woman unslung her pack and sat down on the back section of the fence. Regis, standing over it, looked at her.

"I lied about the girl," she said.

Regis nodded slowly, reverently, his face screwed in concern.

The woman's voice was meek and distant. "It happened at the mall. Exactly… exactly what you warned me about. I locked her in the truck while I went inside. Thought that'd be safer."

Regis folded his arms and considered the quartz.

"I shouldn't have left her. I should have just waited. Waited, like you said." The woman opened her pack to retrieve the purple pouch. She began pulling out small objects: two pink hair barrettes, a pair of green eyeglasses, an action figure, a dog collar, a wedding band, a red crayon, a black crayon, a bead, a picture of two men embracing in paradise.

She took a deep breath, one so deep it seemed to cause her pain. Scorn splashed across her wrinkled brow as she spread the objects out on the ground in front of her. Her eyes glistened, and Regis walked slowly towards her.

She began to say something but brought a hand to her mouth. She bit down on the knuckle of her index finger, and she winced hard.

"Hey," Regis said, "It's okay. It's okay."

She broke, and Regis caught her. She wept there in his arms in the back corner of the graveyard, a small and unimportant place on the edge of the world.

"They're all gone." She sniffled and wiped her nose with her sleeve. "They're all gone."

"I know."

"I was thinking that… Jesus, I'm so bad at this stuff."

"You want to bury them here?"

She nodded. "I don't know if you still pray or anything but I know you used to. I don't really. They never had a funeral. I mean, I know nobody did back then. Still. I don't really know how. I was wondering if you could, I don't know, say something."

The query seemed to smack him in the face, his eyes and his mouth opening wide. He smiled and put a hand on her shoulder. "It would be my honor."

"Really?"

He crouched over the objects, all placed in a line the way a child might survey their toys. "Why don't we start by telling me a little bit about these things? Let's make them real again for a moment before we say goodbye."

"Okay," she said, her voice anything but sure. She picked up the wedding band, a simple gold band that twinkled in the light. "Well, you've seen this before. This was Jason's. I wasn't allowed into the infirmary when the wing took his body. The medic was an E-5, I'll never forget her. She was scared shitless. She gave me his ring back when she told me he was gone. I've had it ever since."

Regis tweezed one of the temple tips of the green eyeglasses and examined it. "Your son's. His name was Bryce, right?"

"Yes. Those are my son's. My son's."

"I met him, didn't I?"

The woman nodded. "He'd be twenty-one now."

"And the hair ties must be your daughter's."

"We lost Jason and Bryce in the same week. Constance and I made it on our own for about a year. I was so devastated when I lost her, so angry. I was alone after that."

She chuckled when Regis picked up the dog collar.

"Of course, I remember good old Georgina," he said.

She chuckled. "She was a good old girl. Thirteen years old. At least I had control over that one. I sure as shit miss dogs, though."

He picked up the picture with a puzzled look. "And who are these guys at the beach?"

She sighed. "A friend. I sort of felt responsible for carrying a piece of him. Same with the crayons and the bead. The crayons were the girl's. The bead belonged to someone I couldn't save."

"Whose action figure is that? Yours?"

"Bryce's. I'm not sure why I still have that. Well, of course I do. I have it because it was his."

"Quite a collection."

She sat placidly over the items, surveying them with her eyes and with her heart. "I had another child not represented here. A baby girl." She looked up at the sky. "Before any of them, there was another one who never even got to see this world. I still think about him, too. At the time, I didn't think the world could be any more cruel. Oh, how I was wrong. My God, that pain. Sometimes I envy him."

They stared at the items together before the woman sighed and gathered them. She pulled a gardening spade from her pack and dug a foot-deep hole into the ground behind the rock. Regis watched her. One by one, she placed the objects inside. She did not cry. With careful motions, she swept dirt over them, patted it down, and held her palms there. She took them away.

Regis knelt across from her.

"Do I have to believe in God for this to work?"

He shrugged and closed his eyes. She looked at him, then closed hers.

"Heavenly Father, we come to you today in awe of your love. We thank you for this day, and for this world, no matter what obstacles lie our path of better knowing your love. We rejoice. We rejoice today as we celebrate these lives."

The woman's hands were shaking.

"But it hurts, Father. Our love for them still shines brightly. Even though we mourn their deaths, we are comforted to know they are seated by your side. We celebrate the love that embraces them. Your love. Bless them, Lord, and keep them close to you. We pray today for the souls of Jason, for Constance, for Bryce, and for all those who we've lost."

Regis paused for a moment to regard an owl staring at them from atop a distant gravestone. Its eyes were clear and bright. It didn't move a millimeter.

"And Father, we ask you to also bless those whose paths still remain unclear. Let us remember that although we may not know the way, we know the destination, and that all roads lead to you. Please, Lord, ease their burdens. Be with them always. Embrace them, Lord, and help them see those faint lights in the darkness. Way out in the darkness. We ask these things in your name, Lord. Amen."

A wind from the east rolled in and cast leaves across the newest grave in the graveyard. Regis clenched his teeth and rubbed his hands together.

The woman opened her mouth to say something, but instead hung her head in silence.

They sat in the calmness of the lengthening day, under the boughs of barren trees cast amongst faded headstones. They sat penitent, like two ancient sages in a runic ceremony, where the souls of all those departed could somehow intermingle. Where they might, for a moment, touch the living.

They were two friends. Two mortals beating back the hooks of extinction, turning away from the darkness, and looking to the light of a faint new dawn.

PART 4

A PATH MOST FAMILIAR

Three days after Regis had left, the woman woke in her bed to the lantern-trill calls of two thrushes outside the cabin. One was strong and one was faint, the nearer bird tweeting from the low branches of a conifer uphill from the cabin.

She dressed and walked to the tree, its leaves tinged white with morning mist. The thrush took two hops down the branch but remained as the woman approached.

"Mating season already?"

As if they were tied to a string, the thrushes' matching songs bounced between the tree and the river until the closer one took flight. It soared across the water towards its new partner.

The woman went down to the river and washed herself. She stared at her reflection, traced the lines branded across her cheeks from over a decade of converter straps. There was color in her face she did not recognize.

While there, she washed the clothes she had on, wrung them, and draped them on a line off the side of the cabin, and then she put on new clothes in the cabin and spent the rest of the day tending the garden. Armed with a machete from the shed, she hacked away at the twisted waste of last year's crop. She pulled the old water jugs out of their mossy holes and brushed them off and returned them to the shed.

She didn't burn a fire that night, opting for a cold dinner, and she spent the evening laying out her most essential belongings on the floor under the light of homemade candles. Their flames danced softly in the errant wind and melted fast the reeking tallow.

Several types of birds screeched and cooed through the evening, magpies mostly, and the woman fell into a deep sleep under her blankets. In the morning, she stuffed her pack her essentials into the bike's saddlebags, and she refilled her four bottles with fresh river water and dropped in iodine tablets.

She sighed as she looked at the cabin — the walls, the roof, the garden, the shed. The meadow, the river, the mountains. The sky, that vast and empty pool of blue possibility, the lingering moon and stars.

An orange flash by the tree line caught her eye. Out of the woods stepped a fox, its nose planted to the ground as it stalked the shrubs there. Three kits trotted along behind it, only the black tips of their ears visible above the grassy border. The woman watched them back into the trees before flicking on the engine.

Her route took her back along a path most familiar, through the rubicund mountain pass towering high above the plains and the lush forest basin. Through spirited wheatfields gleaming with gold and darkened desert prairie where carrion crows caw and whisper. For these were the places that had evolved around her, they that observed her anomalous presence while guarding closely the secrets of tomorrow. They that, like the woman, posited both destiny and doubt upon the world's blank canvas, seeking answers to sacred questions that dwell in the liminal spaces of where all life begins.

Two vehicles passed her on the opposite side of the highway — one a motorcycle flotilla of sorts, the other a van rumbling slowly westward. She stopped for neither, but the driver of the van grinned wide and waved out the window.

Another vehicle passed her, too, when she broke for lunch nearly a hundred yards off the road in the gulch of a rocky creek bed. A mean-looking truck painted all black and decked out with a front grill for ramming, the roar of its engine barely out-screaming its whooping inhabitants, four of them wielding guns and swords as they hung out the bed, hair and robes and headdresses smacking against their painted faces in the wind. The woman watched the truck roll on and spat.

But something arrested her as she entered the wooden haven of Comm 445. It may have been the road's crowdedness, a road typically lined only with guard stations, now bustling with travelers and caravans and characters of all make and mark. It may have been the sights beyond it, people in harnesses strung from ropes on the outer walls dismantling the stalwart timbers that for so long did their best to protect them. Or, it may have been the downright bucolic scene beside her, a group of children and adults swaddled by firelight in the woods, laughing and singing old songs as if the violence that was man's most tireless trait had been unknown to them entirely.

Many in the crowd leered at the woman. Some tried to touch her. Close to the gate, guards sifted through a group of zealots chanting hymns and hawking sloppy theologies. One among them, a leaky-eyed old man with a white, untamed beard, grabbed the inside of her elbow. He spoke odd tongues in a soothsayer's tone, loading each word in his lips to make them more limber. His voice was thin like a snake's, hissing at the woman against the din of the mob.

The woman recoiled and shook him away, knocking down a hobbling old woman in her haste to remount the bike. She shook her arms in her jacket as if to shed invisible vermin from her skin.

Busting through droves of people and vehicles, nearly running them down, she weaved back the way she came on the dirt road and pulled off into a canopy of trees when night fell. She camped deep in the forest, where no one could hear or see her.

And she dreamed that night, dreams so dark and vivid they flowed through her veins, yet it was not their recollection but the pain in her chest that woke her. The knife that would find her in those dreams and lonely moments returned. It was as sharp as ever. It never dulled.

She heaved and clutched her chest. She seethed, squinted, even looked around the tent frantically as if there was something in there she'd lost. Her knees wobbled as she stumbled out, and she groaned and leaned against a tree to vomit.

"I'm coming," she said between frothy and acidic breaths. "Mama's coming."

She took to the road a woman possessed, blazing back onto the highway, chewing up broken asphalt, dodging other vehicles at the highest speeds her bike could conjure. She didn't stop once as she drove through the fields, the forest, or the mountain pass, and she swung onto the turnoff to the cabin so fast her shin scraped the dirt. The bike wasn't made for off-roading, but she drove it anyway down the hill past the cabin, up the north bank of the river, and to the bottom of the hill where the graveyard lived.

The tears pooling in her eyes mixed with beads of sweat as she ran up the hill. She nearly collapsed when she reached the graveyard, but she didn't stop running, and she showed no caution to the headstones between her and the quartz.

Her nails clawed the ground like a dog's. One by one, they appeared, simple objects of metal and plastic, the dirt of the dead lodged in their crevices. With everything back in her hands, even the faded photo, she placed her forehead on the ground and wept. She held the contents of her purple pouch, cradled them, melted into them, the long-lost cells of her own body now returned.

The road took the woman back and forth across the western flank.

She spent many days out on the flatlands, where shelter was sparse amongst the heather and the grain, where skies turned black with the gathering rain. She rode on through the dismal tide across sprawling scrublands and endless seas of prairie, under white-bodied cliffs made pale from desert dust. Higher roads carried her through emerald rows of grass creeping up the sides of snow-tipped mountains, over ruby red canyons made of ancient sediment, around rocky switchbacks pushing up into the heavens. Nights were spent conversing with the stars. Sometimes they spoke back. Sometimes they did not.

Yet no invader did she encounter rolling over the land, no disk in its skies.

She went back to the Crone's compound, now a ruined cinderland, and peered through her binoculars at the skulls still affixed to the spikes that hadn't yet fallen. She passed the place where she'd found Gaff's picked-over corpse, though nothing was left of him now — not a bone, a scrap of clothing, or a trace of his bike. One of the countless billions for whom there was no record.

There was the desert, and Elijah's chimney, and the campground in the valley, and the field behind the barn where she killed the man who raped her. She didn't step foot in the mall but gazed down from the ridgeline at handfuls of people in the parking lot. They conversed and walked freely in and out of the building, as if some semblance of normal commerce had resumed. Some of these places were the same and some of them were different, but all of them were distant to her now, memories mangled by the reshaping of the world and the passage of time.

It was on a crisp spring day, with the sun blazing high between the clouds like a white-hot pearl, that she came to the crossroads with the message board. Both sides were completely blanketed with scraps of cloth and paper. She wheeled her bike off the road, drank a half bottle of water, and one by one began to read them.

A red piece of paper with actual typewriter text stuck out.

CALLING ALL MOTHERLESS SONS AND DAUGHTERS

We seek those that seek a higher purpose.

We quest for the living, we do not mourn the dead.

```
We are the builders, the makers, the
stewards of the human race.

History does not guide our actions, we
look to the future.

Visit the Agency. The place once known
as Comm 971.

Your future begins today.
```

She rubbed her fingers over the scars in her cheeks. As she did, the hum of another motorcycle from the south grew in her ear.

The bike was a tank compared to the woman's, a chopper-style hog with high curving handlebars, a bulky chrome frame, and dual mufflers that looked like silver cannons flanking the chassis. The rider was small — smaller than the woman — and when they took off their helmet, they shook loose deep and curling locks of red hair. She was maybe half the woman's age, face bright yet somehow chiseled with fortitude and weather.

"Hi there," she said, approaching the board. "You a messenger, too?"

The woman took the Crone's message and crumpled it into a ball. "I was for a long time but I stopped. Trying to pick it back up."

"Maybe that's why we haven't crossed paths. I'm a little new at this."

The woman nodded at the chopper. "What kind of mileage you getting on that thing?"

"Could be better, could be worse, I suppose. Wanna trade?" she said with a smile. There was life in that smile, a brightness in her face, a noonday shimmer in her fiery hair.

The woman laughed.

"Have you laid claim to any of these yet?"

"Nah, have at it. I'm not even sure I'm gonna take any. I'm kind of in a weird place with it."

"What kind of place is that?"

The woman bit her lips and gazed out at the skyline as the new rider stepped up to the board. "Hard to say."

"Well, I was thinking about heading south again, so I'm looking for anything addressed to 115 or 662. I might even swing through 354 if that new road's open."

The woman climbed on top of the boulder and sat. "They're all yours."

A soft wind rustled the woman's jacket and tickled the stubble gaps on her head. She gazed out at the great divide, a land simultaneously fractured and thriving, living out its eternal paradox, attempting to regain its consciousness. Attempting to survive.

"I wouldn't mind some company if you're going my way."

"Ah, well," the woman looked away. "I appreciate that. I'm not going that way, though."

With a handful of messages stuffed into her pockets, the younger rider mounted her chopper and fastened her helmet. She pointed to the dirt road that led south. "If I want to get to 115, can I take this all the way? I haven't been that far south before."

The woman looked out over the rider's hand at the dancing wheatgrass. "Yeah."

"You know how far?"

"Probably a two-day ride. Just keep going and you can't miss it."

"Can't miss it?"

"Yeah. Just keep going."

They smiled at each other one more time before the rider took off, and as the afternoon haze dipped over the red crests of the desert, the woman was alone.

After a while, she hopped off the boulder and reviewed the messages again. She noticed one she hadn't seen before, a torn piece of weeks-old paper buried underneath fresher messages.

To: Michelle Johnson, Comm 392

From: Janis Witherspoon, Comm 212

M,

How on earth did you get my message? Someone must be looking out for us.

I’m on my way.

J

You were there to protect me like a shield

Long hair, running with me through the field

Everywhere, you’ve been with me all along

Purse: All that I’ve left behind

The woman read the message again several times. The smile on her face was wide. And it was real.

She kept that small scrap of paper tight between her palm and the handlebar as she got back on the bike.

She rode on.

ABOUT THE AUTHOR

Drew Starling is the author of SENTINEL and NOTHUS, also from Eerie River Publishing. He has received notable praise for his writing, and his works have appeared in a number of anthologies with truly outstanding horror authors. His only rule of writing: the dog never dies.

Reviews are of paramount importance to an author's career, and he would be delighted if you gave this book an honest review on whatever site you purchased it. If you'd like to hear about his upcoming projects, you can join his mailing list by visiting drewstarling.com

CONTENT WARNING

Alcohol use, opioid use, psychedelics use, self-mutilation, suicide attempt/ideation, emotional self-harm, body alteration, starvation, isolation, cannibalism, abduction, enslavement, sexual abuse/rape (women, children), murder (women, children), blood/gore (women, children), animal mutilation (bird).

ACKNOWLEDGEMENTS

This book went through quite a journey to get here. It started as a short story that was rejected by a major indie publisher, and through time and the encouragement of others, grew into the work you've just read. But as Christian Shephard from *Lost* says, "Nobody does it alone," and there are a handful of people who were instrumental in getting this out into the world.

AUSTRIAN SPENCER: You are first on the list for a reason. Without your help, this would still be a short story sitting on the shelf. You have spent more time with this novel than anyone besides me. You have been selfless with your time, honest with your feedback, and true in your friendship. I hope you believe me when I say I could not have done this without you.

ROSS JEFFREY: You were the first author to truly put your weight behind this story, back when it was an initial draft. I've been an admirer of your work for some time now, and I am quite simply honored that you supported me the way you did.

NATE KAYHOE: If there's one thing I've learned through this process, it's that everyone needs a friend who knows everything about cars/motorcycles. The woman's relationship to her vehicles, and the value of good honest work, are major anchors of this story. There's no way in the world I could have done the story justice without your help.

MICHELLE RIVER: Michelle, you are my Ride or Die. You have found ways to get me published since the day I started writing. I brought SENTINEL and NOTHUS to you because I trusted you, and you have never once let me down. I don't know how the heck you do all that you do, but know that I am in awe of you and I am just so delighted that this story — this one that is so personal to me — found its way home to you.

CARA STEVENS: What else can I say to the love of my life? Thank you, my sweet. Thank you for reading all these drafts a thousand times. Thank you for letting me complain to you. Thank you for encouraging me to keep going during all the moments I thought this book was dead, and thank you for trying to persuade me that I'm not a fraudulent writer. Thank you for being you, and thank you for loving me.

EERIE RIVER PUBLISHING

NOVELS & COLLECTIONS

After: Horror Novel by Drew Starling (2024)
The Roots Run Deep: Collection of Horror by C.M. Forest (2024)
A Shadow Over Haven: Nick Holleran Series (2024)
Gulf: Dark Walker Series Book One (2023)
Breach: Dark Walker Series Book Two (2024)
Chasing The Dragon: Horror Vigilante Novel (2023)
The Naughty Corner: Novella Collection (2023)
Shades Of Night: Night Order Series Book One (2022)
Untamed Night: Night Order Series Book Two (2023)
Dead Man Walking: Nick Holleran Series (2022)
Devil Walks in Blood: Nick Holleran Series (2022)
The Darkness In The Pines: Nick Holleran Series (2023)
The Void: Sapphic Fiction (2023)
They Are Cursed Like You: Trailer Park Witches Series (2023)
Infested: Horror Novel (2022)
SENTINEL: The Bensalem Files (2021)
NOTHUS: The Bensalem Files (2022)
Miracle Growth: A Cosmic Horror Novella (2022)
Helluland: Urban Fantasy of Legends (2023)
A Sword Named Sorrow: Fantasy Novel (2022)
Storming Area 51 (2019)

ANTHOLOGIES

The Earth Bleeds at Night: Anthology of Horror
Year of the Tarot: Four Book Series
AFTER: A Post-Apocalyptic Survivor Series
Elemental Cycle: Four Book Series
It Calls From Series
Blood Sins
Last Stop: Whiskey Pete
Of Fire and Stars: LGBTQIA+ Fantasy anthology
From Beyond the Threshold

DRABBLE COLLECTIONS

Forgotten Ones: Drabbles of Myth and Legend
Dark Magic: Drabbles of Magic and Lore

COMING SOON

Seed: Dark Walker Series Book Three (2025)
Infernal Night: Dark Walker Series Book Three (2025)

SENTINEL
DREW STARLING

NOTHUS
DREW STARLING

INFESTED

C.M. FOREST

"'BREACH' LEVELS UP THE SUM OF ITS PARTS, BRINGING EVERYTHING GREAT ABOUT 'GULF' INTO THE FOLD AND AMPLIFYING IT IN THIS NEW REALITY INTRODUCED... FIVE OUT OF FIVE"

-STEVE STRED, AUTHOR OF MASTODON

SHELLY CAMPBELL

BREACH

DARK WALKER SERIES BOOK 2

EERIE RIVER PUBLISHING PRESENTS

THEY ARE CURSED LIKE YOU

TRAILER PARK WITCHES BOOK ONE

HOLLEY CORNETTO & S.O. GREEN

Manufactured by Amazon.ca
Bolton, ON